DISCARDED
BAKER CO. PUBLIC LIBRARY

OCT 22

D1791827

VS Western
Hogan, Ray
Trail of the Fresno Kid

MAR 24 1995

DISCARDED
BAKER CO. PUBLIC LIBRARY

25¢ fine charged
for cards missing
from book pocket

Baker County Public Library
2400 Resort St.
Baker City, OR 97814

DEMCO

TRAIL
OF THE
FRESNO KID

Baker County Public Library
2400 Resort St.
Baker City, OR 97814

Ray Hogan

was born in Willow Springs, Missouri, where his father was a town marshal. When he was five, the Hogan family moved to Albuquerque where Ray still lives in the foothills of the Sandia and Manzano mountains. It was while listening to his father and other old-timers tell tales from the past that Ray was inspired to recast these tales in fiction. What is most impressive about Hogan's Western novels is the consistent quality with which each is crafted, the compelling depth of his characters, and his ability to juxtapose the complexities of human conflict into narratives always as intensely interesting as they are emotionally involving.

TRAIL OF THE FRESNO KID

Ray Hogan

ROUNDUP LARGE PRINT
HAMPTON, NEW HAMPSHIRE

Library of Congress Cataloging-in-Publication Data

Hogan, Ray, 1908–
  Trail of the Fresno Kid / Ray Hogan.
    p. cm
  ISBN 0-7927-2005-9 (hardcover)
  ISBN 0-7927-2004-0 (softcover)
  1. Large type books. I. Title.
[PS3558.O3473T72 1994]
813'.54—dc20

93-48227
CIP

Copyright ©, 1963, by Ace Books, Inc.
All rights reserved

Published in Large Print by arrangement with Donald MacCampbell, Inc. by Chivers North America, 1 Lafayette Road, Hampton, NH 03842-0015

Printed in Great Britain

CAST OF CHARACTERS

Tom Ford
He was a drifter, until they threatened to keep him still for good.

Jay Gordon
He wanted to avenge his son's death and he didn't care how many men got killed in the process.

Bill Tusas
He lived by the code of the bushwhacker: never shoot a man unless he is unarmed, has his back turned and is at least fifty feet away.

Susan Gordon
Her father treated her as a servant, until she got her hands on a shotgun.

Calico Jones
He was getting along in years, but he was in no hurry to die.

Henry Stalcup
He had a glib tongue, but he preferred to make his point with a six-gun.

CHAPTER ONE

The weariness of two years of searching sat heavily on the wide shoulders of Tom Ford. During that time he had ridden the territories and the frontier states in a ceaseless but fruitless quest for his older brother, Fresno. Now, as he looked down from the heights of a craggy, red-faced butte onto the dusty, wind-scoured settlement of Prairie Grove, the thought that had passed through his mind on a hundred similar occasions again moved through him: *Maybe I'll find him here.*

Five years ago, shortly after the war had ended, Fresno had ridden off. He had returned from Manassas, from Chancellorsville, Gettysburg and all the other bloody encounters, more restless and uncertain of his own needs than ever before. Their father, a rigid, iron-willed man, never easy to abide, had taken no steps toward understanding his disquieted son.

There had come bitter, violent clashes; harsh words that could not be unsaid, and in the end Fresno had departed from their Polk County farm in Missouri to disappear into the vastness that was the West.

Tom had heard no more from him directly, but vague rumors had filtered back of a hard-riding, hard-drinking, quick-shooting man called the Fresno Kid. At first he was slow to make the connection and then one day he was visited by a cold-eyed man who made inquiries. The bounty hunter produced a printed dodger, of the sort Tom had seen in the post office, upon which appeared the likeness of a man. The poster declared him to be a dangerous outlaw. He was being sought for certain crimes and a reward of one thousand dollars had been placed on his head.

It was Fresno. There was no doubt of it in Tom Ford's mind. But he disclaimed any acquaintance with the outlaw, realizing in those moments what he must do in the future. The bounty man had gone on, apparently satisfied he had pursued a wrong trail.

Tom had kept the incident from his father, who had grown old from the brutal toil and a secret grieving for his wayward, elder son, and when he died a short time later, Tom came to a decision. There was now no reason why Fresno could not return to his Missouri home. Together they could make a good life for themselves on the farm, far removed from the certainty of death Fresno would one day encounter as an outlaw. In the Polk County hills, lawmen and bounty hunters would never find him.

He had turned over the land to a neighbor,

granting him full use until he returned, and begun the search. It should not be difficult, he reasoned. A man so well known as the Fresno Kid would not be hard to find. But Tom Ford reckoned without considering the lonely, far flung emptiness, the limitless horizons of the country his brother roamed.

For two years he drifted through a world of sparse, scattered settlements, of close-mouthed, suspicious people. He worked when he was broke, searched when he had money in the pockets of his faded Levis to buy food for himself and his buckskin horse. It was a time of many dry camps, of wet sleeps, and too often an empty belly—but he never gave up. There was always another rumor, a new town; and such carried him from Montana to Mexico, from the Indian nations to the golden coast of California.

It was while there he heard of Sutterstown, a settlement lying half in the newly created territory of Arizona, half in Mexico. Beyond the reach of lawmen, it was a haven for outlaws on the run. Tom had ridden there at once, hope again soaring.

He was too late. Discreet inquiry—long ago he had learned a man never asked openly about another, especially one so noted as Fresno Ford—revealed that his brother had been there, and like all others of the transient world in which he lived, had moved on.

Toward the north, so the owner of the *cantina* thought.

The next day Tom was once more in the saddle, following a cold trail that had brought him to a town called Prairie Grove, as the battered, bullet-marked sign sagging from a reeling post proclaimed.

He needed a job. He was down to his last few dollars. He would have to take time out, work, and accumulate another stake, after which he could again resume the quest. But he must find Fresno soon or it would be too late; from what he had learned in Sutterstown, the law was slowly but certainly tightening the net that would ensnare his brother.

Prairie Grove appeared to be no different from the countless other small settlements he had visited in the past. A single, dusty lane fronted by two dozen or so clapboard and *adobe* brick buildings that stood in varying heights and widths along its length. There were two churches, he noted, along with several stores, saloons, livery stables, a Masonic Temple, a hotel with an adjoining restaurant, and a large, sprawling combination dance hall, bar and gambling casino appropriately named the Border Queen. There was a lake, little more than a pond in reality, but in this arid, waterless land of southwestern New Mexico, every body of water was termed a lake.

That there were several ranches and a number of homestead farms in the area was evident from the wagons and buggies and saddle horses halted along the street. He had noted two prosperous looking spreads as he rode in but he did not pause to apply for work. As was the custom he had followed from the beginning, he would first see the town, make the rounds of the saloons, the gambling halls, the livery stables and all such places where men were wont to gather. There was always the slim hope that Fresno would be found in one of them.

Then, if that proved not to be the case, he would go about getting a job. This particular time of year, early summer, it should be easy. Most ranchers were glad to hire on experienced hands at this season and Tom Ford, during the many months he had been on the drift, had become just that; an adept man in many ways, including the use of the heavy, cedar handled Colt .44s that hung low on his hip.

He singled out the hotel, the Great Western, and headed for the livery barn in the rear. He turned the weary buckskin over to the hostler, pulled his blanket roll and saddlebags from the saddle, and started for the hotel.

'You be wantin' this horse again tonight?' the stableman called after him.

'Not tonight,' Tom replied and continued on.

He entered the hotel through a side door, crossed the empty, dust sprinkled lobby, and halted at the desk. A balding clerk looked up at him with no show of interest.

'What'll it be, mister?'

'Room,' Ford said. 'Already put my horse in your stable.'

The clerk shoved a book and a stub of pencil toward him. 'Be a dollar and a half—in advance.'

Ford nodded, began to sign. Because it had been his most recent address, he showed his last residence as Sutterstown. The registration finished, he pushed the dog-eared ledger back to the clerk. The man read the bold, hard slanted script for a moment, then continued to stare at it.

'Something wrong?' Ford asked.

'No sir, Mr Ford,' the clerk said hastily, glancing up. He reached back onto a table. 'Take Number Five—just down the hall a ways,' he said and laid a key on the counter. 'You want to eat you'll find the dining room through that door to your right.'

Tom said, 'Obliged,' and turned about. Five men, several of them much the worse for whiskey, came from the adjoining quarters at that moment. One, a dark, squat rider with powerful shoulders and black, beady eyes, staggered badly. He reeled, tripped over his own spurs and fell against

Ford.

Tom caught him by the shoulders, spun him around and shoved him back at his friends.

'Here's your boy,' he said, a faint smile on his lips. 'Look after him.'

The drunk bellowed, shook off his companions and wheeled about. 'Who you pushin'?' he demanded thickly.

'You,' Tom said, still amused. 'Don't like people stepping on my corns.'

'The hell you say!' the drunk roared. 'Maybe you don't know who you're shovin' around.'

The half smile faded from Ford's lips. 'Don't see that it makes any difference,' he said quietly. He released his grip on his blanket roll, letting it drop to the floor. The saddlebags were still draped over his left shoulder.

The drunk glared at him, his shoulders hunched forward and jaw thrust out. 'Got half a mind to teach you a lesson,' he mumbled.

Tom said, softly, 'Any time you're ready.'

The man standing to the left of the drunk reached out and took him by the arm. 'Aw, come on, Bill. Forget it. Let's go over to the Queen an' get a drink.'

The other chimed in. The squat rider relaxed. He shrugged and shifted unsteadily on his feet. 'All right,' he muttered, 'let's go.'

Ford watched them shamble across the lobby and depart by the front entrance. He bent, picked up his roll, the slight grin again on his face. He glanced at the clerk and winked.

'Must serve mighty powerful liquor around here!'

The clerk, color coming back into his blanched face, nodded. 'That was Bill Tusas,' he said. 'He's a bad one when he's drinking.'

'Sort of gathered that,' Tom replied. 'How's work around here? Anybody hiring on hands?'

The clerk's brows lifted. 'If you're looking for a job, don't reckon you'll have any trouble finding one, Mr Ford.'

'Good,' Ford said and turned into the shadowy hallway to his room. 'I'll be needing one.'

CHAPTER TWO

An hour later, washed, shaved and wearing a fresh shirt, Tom Ford returned to the lobby. He nodded to the clerk, crossed to the door that led into the restaurant and let himself into that area. He paused just inside—a tall, lean man, barely turned twenty but with the cool aloofness of one much older lying upon him.

His eyes, rain gray, were calm, finely drawn by many scorching suns and driving winds; his dark hair, worn long, capped a square cut face. The faint stoop of his shoulders gave him the appearance of wariness, of being forever on the alert for trouble. The open, friendly way that once had been his now shone through only occasionally, for the years had taught him a man must use caution when choosing those in whom he would place his trust.

His flat glance swept the room and touched sharply and briefly the dozen or so men and women gathered there. Part were at the bar, a section partitioned off by a thinly varnished wooden panel, and some occupied the dining room proper with its scatter of tables and stiff-backed chairs.

There were only strangers in the Great Western. When he had determined that fact, his thoughts swung back to the immediate moment. He felt the coins in his pocket. About three dollars remained, he guessed. Not much to go on but a third of it would buy a good meal and twenty-five cents would pay for a couple of drinks at the bar. Anyway, tomorrow he would line up a job.

He moved to a corner table where he could watch the door and see all who came and departed not only the restaurant but the bar as well, then settled down. A hard-faced blonde wearing a lace-edged apron came from the kitchen and served him a glass of cloudy water. Without speaking she waited for him to order.

'Whatever's good,' he said, taking a drink from the glass.

'Special today is beef stew,' she replied. 'That suit you?'

Ford said, 'Fair enough, long as there's plenty of it.'

The waitress swaggered off toward the kitchen. She returned a short time later, bringing his meal. He ate with the relish of a healthy man, one thankful for food prepared by someone other than himself. When he was finished he rose, paid his check and went into the street. The settling coolness of the evening had brought most of Prairie Grove's residents out for a stroll and as he walked slowly along the board sidewalks, he scanned faces carefully. There were only strangers, and when he finally reached the Border Queen, he turned off and pushed through the swinging doors into its interior.

It was well patronized. Tom spent the next hour there, standing at the bar and later drifting aimlessly through the crowd. It was all to no good end. After a time he forsook the noisy tumult and, returning to the street, one by one visited the remaining saloons and similar places of entertainment. Prairie Grove was a busy, active town, he discovered, but Fresno Ford was no part of it. Of that he was dead certain when he headed back for the Great Western.

He went straight to his room, a dingy, wall-papered cell graced by no more than a squeaking bed, a rocking chair with a broken arm rest and a scarred wash stand. But the squalidness did not touch him; it had been much the same pattern in the dozens of other hotel rooms he had occupied during his search across the territories and states.

Removing only his boots and shirt, he stretched out on the bed and almost immediately fell asleep. Moments later, it seemed to him, an insistent knock on the door brought him upright. He had no idea how long he had slept but from the noise arising from the street, he judged it was still early.

He got to his feet, slipped his revolver into the waistband of his Levis and moved nearer the door. He tried to figure who his visitor might be but could come up with no answer. He had made no friends during the evening on his rounds. He remembered then the drunk he had encountered in the lobby; that was a possibility, and his thoughts came to a full stop at that point.

The knock sounded again. He drew off into the dark shadows beyond the bed. 'Who is it?'

'Name's Magee,' a deep voice answered.

'Foreman for the JOG outfit. Heard you were looking for a job.'

The drunk's name was Tusas—Bill Tusas. It could still be some sort of a trick. And it was a little strange that someone should come looking for him to offer a job. He drew his gun, stepped softly to the door and turned the key. Retreating to his position, he said. 'Come on in.'

The panel swung inward. The outline of a tall, slightly stooped man filled the rectangle. He came forward a step.

Ford said, 'Lamp's there on the wash stand. Light it.'

Magee moved deeper into the room and thumped against the rocker. He swore feelingly, located the wash stand and struck a match. Removing the smoky chimney of the lamp he touched the wick with the flame, replaced the glass cylinder and turned around.

'You're a little careful,' he said.

'Old habit,' Tom replied. 'Who told you I was looking for a job?'

'Dunbar—the clerk downstairs. Said you'd mentioned it to him.'

Magee was an older man, somewhere in his late fifties. He had a long face blunted with a stubborn jaw and his hair showed gray below his hat brim.

'You go around looking up men to hire? Didn't know help was that scarce in this country,' Ford said, leaning back against the dresser.

'Always looking for good riders at JOG,' Magee replied. 'Mr Gordon heard about you, sent me in to see you.'

'Gordon? Thought you said Dunbar told you.'

'Well, he told a friend of Mr Gordon's. Then he sent me in to get you.'

'Why didn't this Gordon see me himself?'

'He doesn't get around much. How about the job? You interested or not?'

'Gordon, I take it, owns JOG. Sure, I need a job.'

'Good place to work. Finest spread in the territory,' Magee said, a note of pride lifting in his voice. 'We've got a hundred thousand acres of the best grazing land a man ever set eyes on. Probably would have had more only Mr Gordon got hurt and, like I said, he don't get around much nowadays.'

'Must be quite a place,' Ford commented. 'Whereabouts is it?'

'West of here a few miles. Job pays fifty a month, chuck, a bed, and furnishes the horses. Sound all right?'

'I'll take it, and I'm obliged to Mr Gordon. I'll be there first thing in the morning.'

'I'm heading back,' Magee said. 'Might as well come along with me now.'

Tom studied Magee thoughtfully. The

foreman returned his gaze. After a moment he shrugged, 'Well, I just figured—'

'Sure! Why not?' Ford said then with a laugh. 'Bunk bed couldn't be worse than this one.'

'Be a damn sight better,' Magee declared. 'Pull on your duds and we'll stop at the desk and get your money back. If I know Dunbar, you paid in advance.'

Tom drew on his boots and shirt. He strapped on his belt and holstered his gun. Picking up his saddlebags and blanket roll, he started for the door.

'Always tell a man that's on the move,' the foreman said, a slight edge to his voice. 'Travels light.'

Ford slowed to a halt. 'You got something against that?'

Magee shook his head. 'Nope. Nothing at all. Just was saying it. Now, for me, I like staying put.'

'Man don't always get to do what he likes,' Tom said and walked on out into the hallway.

CHAPTER THREE

In the lobby of the Great Western they halted before the desk. Magee went straight to the point.

'Give Ford back his money. He won't be staying the night.'

The clerk frowned and pushed the steel rimmed spectacles he was now wearing farther up his nose. 'Well, now, I don't know about that, Quint,' Dunbar said.

'Don't give me any argument, Charlie,' the foreman said patiently. 'He's working for JOG ... You don't want me telling Mr Gordon that you—'

Dunbar stared at Magee for a moment, then shrugged. 'All right, Quint. Whatever you say,' he murmured, and tossed the coins Tom earlier had paid him onto the counter.

Magee picked up the money and thrust it at Ford. 'Your horse in the stable?'

Tom nodded. 'Out back.'

'Good. Let's go.'

They paused at the hitchrack long enough for Magee to get his own mount and then walked around the hotel to the squat building standing behind it. The hostler met them at the door. He glanced briefly at Magee and then to Ford, wheeled quickly and disappeared into the depths of the stable. A few moments later he returned with the buckskin, saddled and ready to ride. Tom reached into his pocket for a half a dollar.

'No need for that,' Magee said, swinging to his saddle. 'Tinnin don't mind looking after JOG horses.'

Ford flipped the coin to the hostler anyway and stepped onto the buckskin. It was plain to him by that moment that JOG had great influence in Prairie Grove—and that Quint Magee was taking pride in proving it to him.

Abreast, they entered the town's main street and rode toward its end. All along its narrow length, persons spoke to the foreman, some in friendly fashion, the majority, however, with a sort of respectful caution. When they reached the edge of the settlement and swung west, leaving the lights and clamor behind, Magee turned to Ford.

'Mr Gordon's done a lot for this town. Reckon his business just about supports it.'

Tom Ford nodded. He was still somewhat surprised and mystified by the way matters had been handled. Magee's demonstration of JOG's influence could be put down as pardonable pride in the outfit he ramrodded, but the rest—his approach to hiring, his near insistence that Tom take a job, was difficult to understand. Such procedure was not followed in the case of every hand that went to work for JOG, he was sure. Why, then, for him?

'Gordon got a family?' he asked, after a time.

'Only a daughter,' the foreman replied, and dropped it there.

They continued on in silence after that,

riding at a comfortable lope over the quiet, starlit land that rolled out in gentle waves to all directions. A faint breeze was slipping in from the south, and its touch was cool and refreshing after the day's bright heat. Somewhere an owl hooted softly and Tom Ford was suddenly swept with a longing to settle down in a country such as this, make a place for himself—and forget the endless searching that was gnawing away the years of his life. But in the same breath he knew such was impossible. He must find his brother to offer him the one escape yet possible to him. There was no abandoning his obligation.

'Here we are,' Quint Magee said abruptly.

They had topped out on a low ridge. Below them, in a long, shallow valley lay the Gordon ranch. There was a large main house; a rambling, multi-windowed structure that evidently was quarters for the crew; several lesser buildings and numerous corrals and pens. Lights still burned inside the bunkhouse but the structure where Gordon and his daughter lived was dark.

Riding down the gentle slope, the two riders passed through a tall gate, which had a sign suspended from the cross bar. Magee led the way to a barn where a sleepy-eyed Mexican wrangler appeared and took charge of the horses.

'Boys are still up,' the foreman said, ducking his head at the bunkhouse. 'Might as well name you off to them now.'

They angled back over the hard-pack, entered the long, narrow structure lined with its double decked beds, and halted in the center of the room. The sudden flare of light blinded Ford momentarily but after a time he looked about and saw there were a dozen or so men present. Some were on their blankets, sleeping; one man thumbed through a worn and yellowed magazine; a group played cards at a circular table. All looked up as the two men entered.

Magee waited until he had their attention, including those who were trying to sleep. Then, 'Boys, signed on a new man tonight. Name of Ford—Tom Ford.'

One of the card players shoved back his chair and got to his feet. 'We've met,' he said flatly.

Tom looked more closely at the rider. It was the drunk—back at the hotel. Bill Tusas, the clerk had said his name was. He nodded, grinned, and said, 'We have.'

Tom felt Magee's glance upon him but he made no explanation. He recognized the remaining card players now; they had been with Tusas.

The foreman said, 'Then you know Bill. Rest of the boys at the table there are first, Joe Sharpe. Redhead next to him is Barney Witcher. Then we got Hugh Chesser and last one is Ben Poe.'

Magee paused, shifted his attention to the man with the magazine. 'That's Dan Kirby. Back of him on his bunk is Cletus Todd. Upstairs we got Amos Townsend. Baldy there is Curly Sheppard. And final, there's Calico Jones. He's been around here longer than any other man on the place, except Mr Gordon himself.'

Jones was an oldster, somewhere in his sixties. He had a long, craggy face, beet-red from the sun, and a wispy straggling mustache hung down about his mouth. He bobbed his head at Tom in acknowledgement.

'Got four more men out nighthawking the herd,' Magee said. 'You can meet them tomorrow.' Turning, he moved toward the door, then halted. 'Calico'll show you an empty bunk. In the morning I'll take you in to see Mr Gordon.'

The foreman passed through the doorway out into the yard. In the quiet that followed, Calico Jones said, 'Bed there next to me ain't nobody's. Help yourself.'

Tom, crossing to the bunk, laid his blanket roll and saddle bags across the foot. The smell of trouble hung heavy in the air and he watched Tusas from the corner of his eye. The rider, still slightly drunk, had not resumed his chair. He had pulled back a step and now stood with his legs straddled and thick shoulders hunched forward, studying

Ford with sullen angry intent.

'I ain't said you could sleep in here,' he announced suddenly. 'Take your stuff and get on out to the barn. Be a good place for you—with the horses.'

Tom straightened slowly. It had to come. He had realized that when he saw Tusas. He wheeled about quietly. Calico Jones's feet hit the floor with a soft thud.

'None of that now, Bill! You got no call to—'

'Keep out of this, old man!' Tusas snarled. 'I'm goin' to teach this drifter a lesson he won't forget!'

Ben Poe and the three other men at the table rose and moved back against a far wall. Tusas advanced a step nearer to the center of the room. Ford waited silently.

Jones pushed forward. 'Cut it out now, Bill! You don't need to go thinkin'—'

Bill Tusas's broad hand shot out, caught the old man by the shoulder, and tried to shove him aside. Jones hung on stubbornly. The husky rider's temper flared. His balled fist lashed out. It caught Calico Jones on the side of the head with a dull, meaty thud. The older man went over backward and down to the floor.

'Damn it—keep out of my way!' Tusas yelled and drew back his booted foot to deliver a brutal kick to the old rider's belly.

Tom Ford reacted instantly. Surging in,

he seized Tusas by the collar. He whirled him about and sent him reeling into the wall of the bunkhouse. Something on a nearby shelf dislodged and fell with a noisy clatter.

Tusas, rebounding, recovered quickly. 'Damn you!' he yelled and dragged at his gun.

Tom closed in upon him. He crowded him back against the wall, his own hand clamped on Tusas's wrist. He wrenched the weapon free and sent it spinning into a far corner. Tusas, screaming curses, jerked free, and struck out blindly at Ford. Tom, ducking easily, drove his fist into the cowboy's middle. Tusas gasped, then buckled. Ford caught him squarely with a sharp uppercut that connected with a loud crack. Tusas sank quietly to the floor.

Tom stepped back. He swung his eyes to the four men ranged up against the wall. 'Get him out of here,' he said, his voice low and taut. 'And cool him off before you bring him back.'

Poe and Witcher bent over Tusas and lifted him to his feet. Then, followed by Sharpe and the one called Chesser, they went through the doorway into the night. Ford, tension gone from his lank body, wheeled and dropped to the side of Calico Jones. Todd and the others followed quickly. Tom shook the old man gently.

'You all right?'

Calico, his eyes open, stirred. 'Sure, I'm all right. But you shouldn't 've stuck in your oar. Bill won't be forgettin' what you done.'

'If I hadn't of stepped in he'd have kicked in a few of your ribs,' Ford replied. 'Wasn't your quarrel, anyway.'

'Been a quarrel 'tween us ever since Bill and his bunch went to work here,' Jones said, struggling to a sitting position. 'Once was a good place to work. Sure ain't no more.'

'You better keep an eye on Tusas,' Cletus Todd said then, looking at Ford. 'He'll be sweatin' to even things up with you.'

Tom shrugged. 'I hired on to work, not fight. But if Tusas wants to push it, I'm not the running kind.' He slipped his arms under Calico Jones's shoulders and lifted him to his feet. 'Things are kind of funny around here—like there were two crews—you fellows and Tusas and his bunch.'

'That's hittin' the nail right on the head,' Calico answered, rubbing at his jaw. 'You got them, and you got us. Pick the one you're goin' to side.'

Tom Ford grinned. 'Looks like I've already made my choice,' he said, and crawled onto his bunk.

CHAPTER FOUR

Tom Ford did not hear Bill Tusas and the four men who had departed the bunkhouse after the brawl return that night, but they were on hand for breakfast, red-eyed and worn-looking. They would get little work done that day, Ford thought as he settled down at the long table in JOG's dining quarters.

To his left was Dan Kirby, to the right Calico Jones. Tusas took the chair directly across and several times during the meal Tom caught the squat, dark rider watching him sourly, but he said nothing, simply wolfing his food and gulping his coffee in silence.

Quint Magee put in his appearance just as they were finishing up, evidently having had his breakfast in the separate quarters Gordon provided for his foreman and his wife. Magee halted inside the door and glanced along the table quickly checking off everyone's presence. Satisfied that all were there, he stepped in closer.

'Dan,' he said, touching Kirby with his eyes, 'you and Townsend and Sheppard ride out to the north range. Take along some tools. Bit of fence mending needs doing out there. If you see any stock around, start it drifting back toward the buttes.'

Nodding, Kirby rose to his feet. Townsend and Sheppard followed. The foreman shifted his gaze to Jones. 'Calico, you and Todd, and the new man get on down to the creek. Noticed yesterday grass along there was getting a mite thin. There's a couple hundred head in that pocket. Want you to drive them over and put them with the main herd.'

Calico wiped his chin with the back of a hand. 'Sure, Quint,' he said.

'Bill,' Magee continued, turning his attention to Tusas. 'You and some of the boys ride out and spell off the night crew. I'll send Manuel out with some grub, come noon.'

Tusas mumbled something and proceeded with his eating. Poe and Chesser moved for the door. The men had been separated into distinct crews, Tom noted, Tusas and those who ran with him in one, the older hands in the other. He wondered if this was intention on the part of the foreman or if it just happened to fall that way.

'You about ready?'

Ford became aware of Magee's question, brief, and businesslike. He nodded and pushed back his chair. He started to turn to Calico Jones and explain that he would be delayed for a few minutes but Magee was ahead of him.

'Calico, you and Cletus go on. Ford has to see Mr Gordon.'

The old puncher frowned. 'Ain't he been hired on yet?'

The foreman said, 'Not yet. Come on Ford.'

Tom followed Magee through an inner doorway into a long, dark hall. They walked its length and turned into a room in which were several chairs, a desk, and a cabinet of shelves piled high with papers, magazines and books.

'Have a seat,' the foreman said. 'He'll be here in a minute.'

Almost before Magee finished speaking another door flung back and Jay Gordon, in a wheelchair, propelled himself into the room. He was a large man and despite the loss of the use of his legs, appeared powerfully built. He had snow white hair with brows and mustache to match and his mouth was a tight, colorless line. He looked at Tom with eyes that were hard and glittered with the fire of a mind that drove relentlessly and brooked no opposition. He wheeled himself in behind the desk, never once removing his gaze from the tall cowboy.

'Your name Ford?' he demanded in a sharp, clipped voice.

'Yes, sir. Tom Ford.'

'How long you been around here?'

Gordon would know that, Tom realized. If

the rancher had been told by the hotel clerk of his inquiry concerning work, he would also have been advised that Tom had just ridden in. But he let it pass.

'Just last night.'

'You ever hear my name mentioned before?'

Tom stirred. 'No, can't say that I have. Is it important?'

'I'll say what's important and what ain't!' Gordon snapped. 'You damn sure you never heard it before?'

Anger was beginning to stir within Tom Ford. He shrugged impatiently. 'I've been a lot of places and heard a lot of names. Could have been some Gordons among them. I don't exactly remember.'

'No, I reckon names never mean much to your kind,' the rancher said acidly.

Something within Ford boiled over suddenly. 'Now, what's that supposed to mean?' he demanded, coming to his feet. 'What's this all about? You had me brought out here, saying you wanted to hire me on. If there's no job open say so and I'll keep moving.'

'Sit down!' Gordon barked.

Ford's anger mounted higher. He looked to Quint Magee, standing off to his left. The foreman's face was expressionless.

'Where you been working?' Some of the harshness had left Gordon's tone.

Tom said, 'Arizona—Texas—a lot of places.'

'Understood you came up from Sutterstown.'

Ford nodded. 'You asked me where I'd worked. Didn't hire out down there.'

'Hiding out from the law, eh?'

'No. There's nobody looking for me.'

'Then what were you doing in Sutterstown?'

'Little personal business,' Tom said stiffly. 'And if my being there makes any difference in whether I get a job or not, forget it.'

'You ever up Colorado way, around Creede?'

Tom settled back on the chair. 'Sure. I've been there. Never stayed long.'

'And you didn't run into nobody named Gordon.'

Ford leaped to his feet again. 'To hell with it!' he exploded. 'This isn't the only ranch where a man can get a job.'

'Put him on, Quint,' Gordon said, ignoring Tom's angry words. 'And keep him on,' he added, his eyes boring into Ford. 'Understand this, cowboy; you stay. I hire a man I don't expect him to pull out soon as he gets his first pay.'

'Not so sure I want the job,' Ford said, shaking his head.

Gordon's brows lifted. 'You're looking for work, ain't you?'

'For work, yes, but for all this foofaraw, no. Like all these questions you've been asking. How about you answering one for me? How does it happen you went to all the trouble of sending your foreman after me? You don't know me from Adam and you sure don't hire all your hands like that.'

Gordon's eyes were shrouded. 'Like your business in Sutterstown, something personal. That satisfy you?'

Tom was silent. Gordon's attitude and actions were something he could not understand, but there was an answer somewhere, he knew. It could come from something deep—or it could simply be rantings and ravings of a man once strong and unfettered now consigned to a life in a wheelchair, and taking it out on everyone with whom he came in contact. And he did need the job.

He raised his glance to the rancher. 'It'll do,' he said.

'So be it,' Gordon snapped, his manner again brusque. 'Take your orders from Quint—or from me.' He wheeled away from the desk and halted at the doorway leading into the hall. 'Girl!' he shouted. 'Where's that coffee?'

'Coming, papa,' a woman's voice answered from the far end of the house.

Gordon returned to his desk and sank back in his chair. 'Damn—damn—damn!' he muttered helplessly, pounding savagely at his lifeless legs. 'It's a hell of a thing being crippled up!'

Tom heard quick footsteps in the hallway. A girl, eighteen or so, darkly pretty with chestnut hair and wide set blue eyes, came into the room. She carried a tray upon which were a cup and a small, enameled pot of coffee. She placed it on the desk in front of Gordon, then turned away. She touched Ford briefly with her glance, nodded faintly to Quint Magee and departed.

Gordon looked up at the foreman. 'You got something else on your mind, Quint?'

Magee swallowed quickly. 'Nope, reckon not, Mr Gordon. Everything's going fine.'

'Way it's supposed to go,' the rancher said, pouring himself a cup of black, steaming coffee. 'But it won't if you keep stalling around.'

'Leaving right now,' Magee replied and started for the door.

Ford followed him through the room adjoining to the front, the parlor evidently, and out onto the porch. They halted in the yard. Ford turned to Magee.

'That his daughter?'

The foreman nodded. 'Susan. She sort of looks after him.'

'Treats her a bit rough, I'd say. Like she was a slave of some sort.'

'Never mind!' Magee said, bristling at

once. 'It's nothing for you to be talking about. Jay Gordon's a fine man—it's just that he's all stove in, and he gets a little hard to understand some times.'

'That's for sure,' Tom said. 'Felt like I was up before a judge for murder or something there for a bit.'

Magee gave him an odd look, then smiled. 'Well, you're working for JOG now, and you'd better get to it. Head down that ridge over there to the left and you'll run into Calico and Todd. You know what's to be done.'

'On my way,' Tom said, and struck off toward the corral at a fast walk.

CHAPTER FIVE

An hour later Tom Ford crested a low rise and saw the small herd of beefs Magee had ordered moved. They were drifting slowly across a shallow swale with Calico Jones and Cletus Todd swinging along in their wake.

Astride a close coupled little black he had roped from JOG's branded string, Ford loped down to join the two punchers and assume his part of the chore. As he came up the two men grinned their welcome and then Todd pulled out circling the stock and pointing for the hills to the west.

'Clete's gone to locate the rest of the herd,' Jones explained. 'Ain't sure whether it's south of us or to the north. Was about to give you up.'

Tom turned himself sideways on his saddle, hooked one leg over the horn, and settled himself comfortably. He pulled tobacco and papers from his shirt pocket.

'Had quite a talk with Gordon,' he said, offering the makings to the old puncher. 'Still don't know exactly what it was all about.'

Calico glanced at the tobacco, shook his head. 'One habit I ain't got,' he said. 'How'd you make out with Jay?'

Tom rolled himself a thin cylinder, sealed it and thrust it between his lips. 'Not sure. I'm working. That's about all I can say.'

A half-a-dozen steers broke suddenly from the herd, and veered off to one side. Jones raced after them, expertly hazed them back into line, and returned to his position beside Ford.

'That's good,' the old puncher said, resuming the conversation. 'Jay's all right. Just got hisself soured down some since he got hurt. Then it got worse when his boy got killed.'

'Boy? Didn't know about that.'

'Happened a couple years ago. Boy's name was Jock. Watched him grow up myself. Jay had hopes he'd learn the business and take over the ranch someday, but it just didn't work out that way. One thing, Jay spoiled the boy somethin' fierce. And he was wild as a March wind. Then along come the war. Jock was no more'n seventeen. Run off and joined up in spite of what his pa said.

'Got through it all right, howsomever, but when he come back there was no holdin' him. Restless and jumpy as a bull in a slaughter chute. He hung around the place for a month or so, then one night he just up and disappears. Next thing we heard he'd got in a shootin' scrape up north somewheres and got hisself killed.'

'Who did it?' Tom wondered.

'Don't know myself. Jay never talked about it none. He sent Quint Magee up to look after things. Reckon he must have told Quint to keep his trap shut 'cause he never said nothin' either. Since then Jay just goes along actin' like Jock never was, but he don't fool me none. He's plenty bitter about it, and keepin' it all locked up inside hisself makes him mighty hard to abide.'

'Figured something was chewing at him. What kind of a man is this Magee?'

'Quint? Straight as a rail. Don't believe in nothin' but JOG, and whatever Jay Gordon tells him is blue fire law far as he's concerned. He's got a wife but you'd never know it, 'cause he eats, sleeps, drinks and lives for this here ranch—and nothin' else.'

'Thing that bothers me,' Ford said, squaring himself again on his saddle, 'is how they hired me on. Never had a man look me up and plain, outright offer to hire me before. Just about insisted on it. Sure can't be because I'm such a good cow nurse. Lots of men better than me.'

Jones studied Ford thoughtfully. 'Ain't no tellin' what the reason is. Jay does things funny sometimes—like hirin' on Bill Tusas and his bunch. They don't come no ornerier than them. Once heard Jay say a rancher had to have a few hardcases on his payroll just to keep other hardcases and rustlers off the place... Reminds me, never did give you a proper thankin' for pullin' Tusas off me last night. I'm obliged but you didn't need to bother. I been slapped around by him before. Just about everybody but Jay and Quint have. I reckon.'

'He's tough, no doubt of that,' Tom agreed.

'And somebody you'd better keep watchin'. He won't be forgettin' what you done to him.'

Ford nodded. 'I've run up against his kind before. I'll watch him. Where'd he and the others go last night? Never did hear them come in.'

Calico shrugged his bony shoulders. 'Hard tellin'. They pull off like that ever' now and then. Gone most of the night, as a rule, but they always show up for breakfast and ready to work. Bein' close to town, I expect they go in and do a little drinkin' and hell raisin'.'

'Doesn't Magee ever jump them about it?'

'What for? Long as they're fit to work, ain't much he can say.'

They rode along in silence after that. The herd moved slowly, following out a long, broad swale that grooved a green path toward the mountains to the west. The morning was warm, pleasant, with the day's harsh heat yet to set in.

'Todd ought to be showin' up,' Jones said, finally breaking the lull, 'unless the herd's farther north than I figured. Place is dang nigh too big to handle right.'

'Hundred thousand acres, so Magee told me.'

'And all of it prime grazin' land. Shape it's in Jay could do with less.'

'That's a change,' Tom commented. 'Most places I've worked for the owner was always reaching out to grab more.'

'Not Gordon. Heard him say plenty of times he had all the grass he wanted, that it was hard enough to take care of what he already owned. Especially in winter. Get some mighty bad snows here now and then.'

'You been with Gordon long?'

'Longer'n anybody, like Quint said. Fact is, I was with Jay when he bought his first little jag of cows. Seen him start with about nothin' and build it up to what he's got now. Was around when the kids was born, and when his wife died. He like to lost everythin' that year. Had a real old time blizzard. Half the herd froze to death, and with losin' his wife and all, I didn't see how Jay could keep goin'. But he did.'

'It's a fine spread,' Tom murmured. 'Can't think of ever seeing one any better. Easy to understand why you've stayed on.'

Calico Jones bobbed his head. 'You done a big spell of driftin'?'

Ford said, 'Quite a bit.'

'Don't mean to be nosy,' Jones said. 'Just that I'm a talker—one thing an old man can do. And it sure gets lonesome out here in the flats and hills once in awhile.'

'It's all right,' Tom said. 'Been on the move since right after the war. Got a brother out in this country somewhere and I'm trying to find him. We've got a farm back in Missouri and I figured if I could locate him, we'd go back and start farming again. You ever hear of a man with the same name of Ford—Fresno Ford?'

Jones clawed at the stubble on his chin. 'Nope, can't recollect ever comin' across it before. You're the first. You ain't got no idea where he'd be?'

'None. Pick up a rumor ever' so often, but I'm always too late.'

'What's he do?'

Tom Ford thought for a long moment. Then, 'Just a drifter, same as me.'

Calico nodded his understanding. 'Way it is with plenty of young bucks since the war. Just couldn't make themselves settle down. You do any fightin'?'

'No. Had to stay on the farm with our pa. My brother joined up with Forrest.'

'War sure changed a lot of things. And there's a lot of men who never got hit with a musket ball or took a saber slash that got hurt bad just the same. Thing like all that killin' does somethin' to a man's mind, changes his way of lookin' at life...'

The old puncher paused, his eyes reaching beyond the herd. A lone horseman was coming down the slope toward them. 'That'll be Clete,' he said.

Todd wheeled in beside them. He grinned at Ford, then placed his attention on Jones. 'Herd's about five miles off. Better start slantin' north.'

Calico said, 'Fine. Beginnin' to feel a might gaunt. Breakfast sure didn't stay with me. They got the grub yet?'

'Yeh. Bill and the others have done eat. Told them to leave some for us.'

Todd, his face going serious, turned to Tom. 'Might be a good idea was you to cut back to the ranch, son. Me and Calico can handle the stock from here on.'

Jones glanced at his partner. 'Why?

Trouble brewin'?'

Todd said, 'Sure is. Bill said for me to tell Ford he was waitin'—that he wanted to take up where he left off last night.'

'That danged Tusas!' Calico exploded, 'always spoilin' for a fight. You better do like Clete says, Tom, and head back for the ranch. Out here Bill will have everythin' his way.'

Ford was silent for a moment. He shook his head. 'No point to dodging it. Only come again later.'

Calico Jones shrugged. 'Might've knowed you wouldn't run,' he said. 'But you watch yourself. Bill will try anythin'. Me and Clete will back you all we can.'

'Thanks,' Tom answered. 'Just keep the others off my neck. I'll take care of Tusas.'

CHAPTER SIX

It was near two o'clock when they reached the herd. The cattle were spread out over the floor of a vast, green basin, the exact center of which was marked by a small, spring fed lake, which reflected the sky with its white, fleecy clouds like a deep mirror. As they drew closer Tom could see Bill Tusas and his men lounging in the shade of a cottonwood tree that grew half way up the yonder slope.

'Reckon that finishes our chore,' Calico Jones said as the steers they were driving caught scent of the water and began to run. He mopped at his brow and threw a glance at Ford. 'Could turn around and head for the ranch,' he added.

Tom shook his head and continued on toward the spreading cottonwood. Jones and Todd fell in beside him, and together they rode on.

Tusas, surrounded by Sharpe, Barney Witcher, Ben Poe and Hugh Chesser, watched their approach in silence. A blackened pot hung over a low fire and beyond it was a wicker basket in which sandwiches and other items of food had been delivered.

'Coffee smells mighty good,' Jones said with false cheeriness as they pulled to a halt. 'And I can sure use some of them sandwiches.'

Neither Tusas or the others made any comment. Tom feeling his nerves grow taut, came off the saddle, ground reined his pony with the rest and started for the fire.

He reached it at the same time as Jones and Todd and picked up one of the tin cups. He held it out while Calico filled it from the pot.

'Sure is hell when they make a man eat with a stinkin' saddle tramp,' Tusas drawled from his position under the tree. 'Can't hardly keep my mind on my work.'

'Same here,' Poe said. 'Kind of turns my stomach.'

Tom Ford sipped slowly at the steaming, strong coffee. But within him tension and anger was beginning to lift. Tusas was determined to push him into a fight, there was little doubt of that. At first, when Cletus Todd had warned him of it, he thought it would be wise to accept the promise and get it over with. Now, facing Tusas and the four toughs who would side him, he was not so certain. They would never let Bill lose. He knew he could count on Calico and Todd, but they were older men; they could not be expected to stand up against Poe and the others.

'You figure I ought to do somethin' about it?' Tusas went on in his dry, sardonic way.

'Your bounden duty,' Barney Witcher declared. 'Up to you to keep things nice around this here ranch.'

Calico Jones got to his feet. Wheeling about, he glared at Tusas. 'Don't be tryin' to start somethin' here, Bill! Ford ain't botherin' you none, and he's welcome around this here camp same as any man workin' for JOG. Just you leave off tryin' to rawhide him into a ruckus.'

'Shut up, old man!' Tusas snarled, suddenly angry. 'Told you to mind your own business last night. This here is between me and the drifter. Ben—hand me your rope.'

Poe moved quickly to his horse and pulled the coiled lariat from his saddle. He tossed it to Tusas. 'What you figurin' to do?'

'Barney just told you—up to me to keep things cleaned up around here. I'm goin' to drag him off where he won't be smellin' up things.'

Tom Ford came slowly around. His face was stiff, a shade whiter. 'Take my advice, Bill—forget it.'

Tusas halted. Throwing back his head, he laughed loudly. 'You hear that, boys? He's tellin' me to forget it! Put your gun on him, Barney, while I get this rope throwed over him.'

Witcher drew his pistol and moved up close to Tusas. Calico Jones muttered something, then stepped back from the fire. Todd followed. Again Tusas paused. He looked at the two old men speculatively.

'You takin' a hand in this? One thing you had ought remember—you do and you'd better figure on leavin' with the drifter when I'm done with him. This ranch won't be no healthy place for either of you.'

'You ain't scarin' me none!' Calico declared stoutly. 'If they's got to be a fight, it's goin' to be a fair one.'

'Keep out of it,' Ford said in a low voice, never taking his eyes off Tusas. He still held his cup of coffee, half empty, in his left hand.

Tusas, flanked by Witcher, eased forward slowly. He had formed a loop with the rope and had it extended preparatory to tossing it over Ford's shoulders.

'Telling you once more, Bill,' Tom murmured. 'Forget it, or—'

'Or what?' Tusas yelled and threw the loop.

Ford sidestepped nimbly. In the same flashing instant he tossed the coffee, cup and all, into Witcher's face. He lunged for Tusas, caught him by the arm and jerked hard. As the squat rider stumbled by Ford sent a smashing blow into his head.

Pain shot up Ford's arm, clear to the shoulder, as the two men crashed together, but there was no time to pause. Tusas, clawing for him as he went to his knees, caught Ford by the leg, and dragged him to the ground. Tom sprawled flat. Tusas was on him instantly, hammering mercilessly at his face and neck.

Ford heaved upward, spilled the husky man to one side, and rolled free. He leaped to his feet, anger a wild, surging force racing through him now. He whirled on Tusas, coming up fast. He met the rider with a straight left that rocked the man to his heels. He followed with a whistling right that traveled a full arm's length. It caught Tusas on the ear and drove him to his knees. But the man would not stay down. He was up and boring in almost immediately.

Tom danced away. Tusas was strong—and he could absorb an amazing amount of punishment. He had demonstrated that fact by rising quickly after being felled by two shocking blows.

Ford halted abruptly, then stung Tusas with a sharp left to the mouth that drew blood. The rider yelled in fury and surged forward. He surprised Ford with two hard blows to the ribs that drove the wind from his lungs.

Springing away, Ford hurled himself beyond reach of Tusas's clawing fingers. He wheeled, caught the man off balance, and smashed him with a wicked right to the jaw. Tusas wavered uncertainly. His arms dropped to his sides and his brow knotted into a frown. Ford moved in swiftly, spun the man about with a hard left, and smashed him to his knees with a murderous right.

Tusas, supporting himself with his arms, shook his head savagely, then struggled to throw off the fog that engulfed him. Ford stepped back, waiting. Beyond the fallen man he could see Barney Witcher, gun still in hand. Farther back were Poe and Joe Sharpe and the lean-faced Hugh Chesser. They looked on with a wild sort of fascination filling their eyes. His back was to Calico Jones and Todd. He could not see what they were doing—or even if they were still there. He brought his gaze back to Tusas.

'You had enough?'

'No—by God!' the squat rider yelled, lunging forward.

Ford stepped back hastily, and felt the entangling coils of Tusas's rope, dropped at the beginning of the fight, wind about his ankles. He took a faltering step, tripped and fell hard.

He heard Bill Tusas shout triumphantly as he was going down. He saw the man loom over him, saw his booted foot descending to crush his face. He jerked aside, throwing up an arm to protect himself. His fingers came in contact with a spur. The tines of the rowel gashed into the palm of his hand. He winced, ignored the pain, and jerked.

Tusas yelled again and went crashing to the ground, flat on his back. Ford, kicking his feet free of the rope, scrambled to an upright position. Tusas, blood smearing his face, rolled to one side.

'Gun him down!' he screamed at Witcher. 'Shoot him, damn it.'

Tom Ford wheeled and drew in a single, fluid motion. His gun cracked in unison with that of the redhead's. He felt the searing pain of a bullet gashing across his leg and went to one knee as reflex action released his muscles.

He saw Barney Witcher spin about. His pistol hung limply in his hand and there was a dazed, surprised look on his face. Suddenly his legs buckled and he collapsed into a heap.

There was dead silence. Tom Ford waited while Tusas got to his feet and walked to where Witcher lay. Poe and Chesser moved up with him. Sharpe, alone, did not stir. Chesser, kneeling beside the redhead, examined him briefly. He glanced up at Tusas.

'Smack through the heart.'

From behind him Ford heard Calico Jones swear softly and then say, 'Reckon you ought to be satisfied, Bill. You got a man killed here today.'

Tusas spun about angrily. His face was taut, his eyes hard. 'Not me, old man!' he snapped. 'I didn't kill nobody. It was that damn drifter there who pulled the trigger—and don't none of you forget it!'

CHAPTER SEVEN

Ford, breathing heavily from exertion, gun still in his hand, watched Tusas narrowly. After a time he spoke.

'What about it, Bill?' he asked softly. 'Do we go on from here?'

Tusas glared at him. Pure hatred shone in his eyes, flattened the planes of his dark face, set the muscles of his jaws to working spasmodically. And then he shrugged.

'Later,' he muttered.

'No better time than now,' Ford said in a quiet, deadly way. 'Odds are all with you.'

The squat rider turned away abruptly. 'Nope—you ain't ramrodding me into no showdown—not when I ain't ready. Let's go,' he added curtly to the men behind him.

Poe took a half step forward, hesitated. 'What about Barney?'

'Up to the drifter,' Tusas said without halting. 'Let him explain it to the law—and to old man Gordon.'

They moved to their horses and swung to their saddles. Jerking about, they whirled off toward the north. Tom Ford watched them go as the hard pressures and tensions began to fade from his body. The muscles of his arms and shoulders slowly relaxed. He pulled himself upright, came about and faced Calico Jones and Todd. He felt a deep, breathless sickness in the pit of his stomach and a great weariness settled over him. As if from a distance he heard Jones speak.

'Don't you go worryin' none, Tom. Dorsett's a fair man, and you got us to back your story. You didn't have no choice.'

'Dorsett?' Ford echoed the name blankly.

'The marshal—at Prairie Grove,' Todd

explained. 'Art's all right but I ain't so sure how Gordon'll take it.'

'The hell with Gordon!' Ford snapped, abruptly impatient. 'I suppose he'd like it better if it was me lying there.'

'Didn't mean it that way,' Todd said hurriedly. 'He just plain don't like gunplay on the ranch.'

'Somebody should have told Witcher that,' Ford said drily. 'How far are we from town?'

Calico Jones looked out across the hills. 'Maybe ten miles, was you to head direct south. Why?'

Ford walked toward the horses. 'I'm taking Witcher's body in and turning it over to the marshal, and telling him what happened.'

Todd nodded approvingly. Calico plucked at his chin. 'Might be smarter, was I to do it.'

Tom shook his head. 'No, it's my responsibility. Best the law gets it first hand. However, if I'm not back at Gordon's by noon tomorrow, you can figure this Dorsett didn't believe my story and locked me up. Appreciate your riding in then and straightening things out.'

Calico bobbed his head. 'We'll do it. And we'll tell Magee the way of it. He'll want to know.'

They loaded Witcher's body onto his horse and tied it securely to the saddle with a thong. Ford, mounting his own pony, took the lead rope from Todd.

'Due south,' he said, repeating directions.

Jones said, 'Right, and straight as a crow flies. And maybe you'd better keep your eyes peeled for Tusas and them others. They could hatch up more devilment.'

'Wasn't for somebody havin' to stay with the herd, it'd be a good idea for us to ride along,' Todd said.

Tom grinned at the two oldsters. 'Forget it. I'll make it all right. So long.'

He started up the long, gentle slope at a walk, Witcher's horse hanging back and not taking kindly to the rope. When he reached the crest Tom Ford looked back. Jones and Cletus Todd were still standing near the cottonwood, their eyes following him. It was almost as if they feared his going, that they were afraid more trouble lay ahead for him.

And they could be right, he thought grimly. Tusas, burning with hate and anger, could be expected to seek his revenge. He might pull an ambush, or even an outright attack since the odds would be four to one.

Involuntarily, Tom Ford half turned on his saddle and swept the hills with a quick, searching glance. There were no riders in sight. Even Calico and Cletus Todd were hidden from view now. But it was best he be on his guard. He looked toward the sun. It was still fairly high in the steel blue arch of the sky, and that was one thing in his favor; he would reach Prairie Grove before dark.

Matters had taken a swift turn since he had ridden into the valley in quest of Fresno and now, as he rode slowly along, he was beginning to have doubts as to the wisdom of staying on. He had sought only to work, to accumulate a little money and then ride out; but suddenly he had been caught up in trouble—something he had made a rule to never seek, yet just as steadfastly refused to run from when it was thrust upon him.

And Jay Gordon. He still could not understand the actions and the thinking of the rancher. It was almost as though Gordon, for some special reason, wanted him to work for JOG. Just why was not clear and he reckoned the smart thing to do was to accept it, to do his job and earn his pay. It would be stupid to let Bill Tusas or anyone else deprive him of the opportunity.

His thoughts came to a halt. A lone rider had moved into view on a long ridge a quarter mile ahead. Tom watched the man intently, striving to recognize him. The distance was too great for positive identification but after a time he decided it was not Tusas or one of his crowd.

He continued on, not breaking pace. He settled himself a bit more squarely in the saddle and shifted his holster forward until his gun was more easily available. He noticed the seared wound on his leg at that moment, having forgotten it almost from the instant Barney Witcher's bullet had carved its stinging groove. It had bled some but not seriously. He would get the doctor to bind it up for him when he got to town.

The horseman was a stranger. He was an older man, round-shouldered, gray-haired and with a heavily seamed face. He halted at the foot of a low hill and watched Tom approach with sharp, calculating eyes.

As Ford drew to a stop a few paces from him he nodded, said, 'Howdy. Appears you've had yourself a mite of trouble.'

Tom said, 'Some,' and fell silent.

'Name's Gillen,' the stranger said. He shuttled a glance at Witcher's body. 'Friend of yours?'

'Not exactly,' Ford replied. 'Taking him in to the marshal.'

'I see. Looking for the Gordon ranch, myself. Am I headed right?'

'Keep going east, you'll run into it.'

Gillen's face suddenly stiffened. His eyes hardened as they studied the pony Ford was riding. He looked at Tom accusingly.

'That's a Gordon horse. Wearing a JOG brand. You one of his hands?'

Ford said, 'I work for him.'

'Should have guessed it!' Gillen muttered. 'Seeing the dead man, I should have guessed it.'

'Meaning what?'

'Meaning that when there's been a killing you can figure Gordon and his outfit will be mixed up in it!'

'Gordon had nothing to do with it.'

'Don't tell me that!' Gillen exclaimed, suddenly agitated. 'Killing and burning is all Gordon knows. He's been pulling it around here for more'n a year now. Some of his renegade help hit the farm next to mine just last week!'

'Gordon? Jay Gordon?' Ford said disbelievingly. 'Mister, you got your ropes crossed somewhere!'

'Like hell I have! You think I don't recognize a JOG brand? You think I haven't seen it before? I've seen it plenty on the horses of the riders who've been raiding our places, burning the houses, shooting and tearing things down. Every night I've been wondering if I was next on the list—listening and watching, until I'm half crazy from it. Well, I'll tell you this, and you can put it in your pipe and smoke it, Gordon ain't getting my place. I won't run or sell out. He'll have to kill me!'

Tom Ford listened to the wild torrent of words in amazement. There had to be some mistake. Gordon wasn't interested in more land—Calico Jones had said so and Tom believed the old puncher because it made sense. JOG had no need for more range.

'Still think you're wrong,' Ford said. 'Of course I've only been working for him a short time.'

'How long?'

'About a day.'

'One day!' Gillen shouted. 'Then you don't know the first thing about what's going on! ... I'll give you some advice—ride on out unless you want to find yourself mixed up in the worst damn range war this country has ever seen.'

'Range war?'

'Right! Gordon maybe can run off some of the little ranchers and homesteaders and get their land for near nothing, but there's a few of us who won't scare. We've joined together and we're going to fight. I'm on my way now to see Gordon and tell him so. Either he pulls in his guns and quits it—or we're doing a little raiding and burning on our own.'

Ford shook his head. 'Makes no sense to me,' he said. 'What about the law? Why don't you get them in on it if you're so sure?'

'Law's no use to us. First place the marshal in Prairie Grove won't buck Gordon. He won't even listen to us. Next thing, we're all over the county line, west of here. Dorsett's got no jurisdiction there even if he had guts enough to help us. And there's no sheriff or marshal in our county. Hell, there ain't even a town—just a few ranches and farms. Have to do our trading in Rock

Springs, a place in the country south of us.'

Ford considered for a long minute. He shrugged finally. 'Got to be a mistake somewhere. Expect you'll find that out when you talk to Gordon. This,' he added, motioning toward Witcher, 'was a personal matter. Had nothing to do with anything like you're talking about.'

Gillen made no immediate answer. 'So ... well, no difference to me,' he said then. 'If he was one of Gordon's renegades, simply means it will be one less we'll have to face if it comes down to a fight.'

'You're all wrong,' Tom replied stubbornly and touched the black with his spurs. 'You'll see I'm right when you meet up with him.'

Gillen favored him with a cold glance. 'You think so? Ride over to the valley someday. I'll show you a few burned out houses—and some fresh graves. Then we'll see if you're so blasted sure.'

'Might be true,' Tom said without slowing down, 'but it doesn't prove Gordon had anything to do with it.'

'No? Then I'll show you the hide of a horse that's nailed to my barn. One of the raiders was riding it when I shot it out from under him. It's wearing a JOG brand on the left hip, just like that black you're forking,' Gillen said, and moved on.

CHAPTER EIGHT

It was shortly before sundown when Tom Ford rode into Prairie Grove. He traveled down the center of the solitary street, angling for the marshal's office at the far end of the structures. A crowd began to gather quickly and by the time he reached the lawman's quarters two dozen or more persons were trailing along in his wake.

'Who is it?'

He heard the half whispered, excited question voiced over and over and when he swung from the saddle, one man stepped up and peered closely at the corpse. He fell back in surprise.

'Barney Witcher! What happened?'

Tom ignored the question and turned toward the man coming from the marshal's office. Art Dorsett was well on in his sixties. Erect, a neatly trimmed beard and mustache, fairly well dressed, he wore his lawman's badge proudly. He placed his sharp eyes on Ford.

'What's this, mister?'

'Barney Witcher's body. He tried to kill me. I was a little faster.'

Dorsett's gaze touched the blood stained tear in Ford's Levis. 'Not too much faster, I'd guess. Who're you?'

'Name's Tom Ford. Working for Gordon at JOG.'

Dorsett nodded. He glanced over the crowd. 'Rufe, take the body over to Appleton. Tell him I said to look after it. You,' he added, coming back to Ford, 'step inside.'

He wheeled about and Tom followed him into the small office. It was a single room almost filled by a desk and four or five chairs. Leading off it was a hallway that provided access to the barred cells at the other end of the building. Dorsett dropped down behind his desk.

'Have a seat, Ford,' he said.

Tom settled himself in one of the rigid, straight backed chairs. Dorsett drew a sheet of paper from the top drawer of his desk and made several notations with a pencil. Then he looked up.

'Don't recollect seeing you around here before. How long you been working for Gordon?'

'Hired on last night. My first day.'

'Didn't take you long to get into trouble,' Dorsett said caustically. 'How'd it happen?'

Ford shrugged. 'Was having a little argument with Bill Tusas. Witcher horned in—with his gun.'

The lawman wrote something on the paper. 'There anybody else around that saw all this?'

'Calico Jones and Cletus Todd. And the bunch that runs with Tusas.'

Dorsett leaned back in his chair, nodding vigorously. 'If Calico backs your story, then it's good enough for me. But I reckon you'd better spend the night here.'

Ford's face clouded. 'You locking me up?'

The marshal looked surprised. 'You don't expect me to turn you loose right off hand do you? The country ain't going to miss Barney Witcher none, but it was still a killing. Expect what you told me is the truth but I'll have to hear it from Calico, too.'

Ford said, 'How long will I have to stay here?'

'I'll ride out to Gordon's tonight. If everything's all right you'll be out in the morning. Be a good idea for you to sort of stay off the street anyway, until Bill Tusas cools off. You're not thinking this is over yet, are you?'

Ford shrugged. 'Far as I'm concerned it is.'

'Then you got Tusas figured wrong.'

Tom said, 'Could be. Any chance of turning me loose long enough to get my leg doctored up? And I'd like a bite to eat.'

'I'll take care of it,' Dorsett replied. 'Give me your gun.'

Ford rose and unbuckled his belt. He laid it on the desk before the lawman. Dorsett slid it into a top drawer, then resumed making out his report. Tom settled back in his chair again.

'Marshal, you hear any word on a range war that's brewing around here?' he asked, after a time.

Dorsett did not look up. 'Range war? Nope, nothing that I know of. Why?'

'Ever hear of a rancher named Gillen?'

'Sure. Got a little spread west of here, in the next county.'

'Ran into him this afternoon. Claims Gordon has been pulling some raids over in his part of the country, burning out homesteaders and small ranchers. Was on his way to tell Gordon that if he didn't quit it, there was going to be big trouble.'

Art Dorsett had stopped writing. 'What do you think about it?'

'Told him he was wrong. From what I hear Gordon's got all the range he wants.'

'Way I look at it, too. I've heard those rumors before. Never put no stock in them. Maybe there is some trouble going on over there, but it could be most anybody behind it. Little ranchers always blame the big ones.'

'Gillen was pretty sure. Said he even had the hide of a JOG branded horse killed during one of the raids to prove what he says.'

Dorsett stared at Tom. 'What's all this leading up to, Ford? You think Gordon is out to drive off all the homesteaders and small cattlemen?'

'No, but I think somebody better be looking into it. Gillen was plenty riled over something. And unless it gets straightened out my guess is you'll have one hell of a ruckus on your hands before long.'

'Maybe you're right,' the lawman said. 'But I don't figure Gordon's got anything to do with it. There's some other answer. I'll talk to Jay about it when I get out there.'

The lawman finished his writing, then rose to his feet. He motioned toward the hall. 'I'll lock you up now,' he said. 'Then I'll see about getting the doc over here and rustling you up some grub.'

Ford got up, turned about and walked to the first of the cells. There were only two and both were empty. He entered, sank down on a cot. Dorsett slammed the door and twisted the key.

'Back in a few minutes,' he said and wheeled off.

The doctor returned first. He was a short, bald man with steel-rimmed spectacles perched on the tip of his nose. He fidgeted impatiently until Dorsett showed up, carrying a napkin-covered tray of food.

It took the physician only a short time to clean and dress the wound in Tom's leg, declaring it to be no more than a scratch. And then he was gone.

'I'll be riding to Gordon's now,' the

lawman said, setting the tray on the end of the cot. 'Just make yourself comfortable 'til I'm back.'

Ford glanced around the barren cell. 'Comfortable,' he echoed wryly. 'Be a little hard to do.'

Dorsett grinned, made no answer. He left and moments later Ford heard him ride out. He finished his meal of steak and potatoes and coffee, placed the tray on the floor and stretched out on the hard bed. The sounds of the town died gradually, and then suddenly sunlight was streaming through the window and Marshal Art Dorsett was standing before him.

'Calico and Todd backed you right down the line,' the lawman said cheerfully. 'Reckon you're free to go anytime you want.'

Ford drew himself upright. 'Good . . . How about that other matter? You talk to Gordon?'

'Nope. He was sleeping when I got there and I didn't want to roust him out. Guess you must have got things a little crossed, anyway.'

'Crossed?'

'Yeh. Gillen or nobody else ever showed up at Gordon's yesterday.'

CHAPTER NINE

Ford studied the lawman's bland features. 'You sure of that?'

'Sure as I can be. Asked several of Gordon's boys. Nobody saw any visitor.'

Tom walked slowly to the office area of the jail. He stood by silently while Dorsett fished out his gun and belt, and handed them to him. 'Must have changed his mind,' he murmured, strapping on the weapon.

There was no comment from the marshal. Tom glanced at him and read the doubt in the man's eyes. 'You don't think I saw Gillen at all, do you, marshal?'

Dorsett shrugged, leaned back against the edge of his desk, and crossed his arms over his breast. 'You say you did. I don't call you a liar, but I know that Gillen or nobody else rode into Gordon's anytime yesterday or last night.'

A quick answer shaped up on Tom Ford's lips, and then he stifled it as realization and truth came to him. He had not been dreaming. There was a man named Gillen and he had been on his way to see Jay Gordon. *He simply had not reached his destination.* Either he had altered his plans, which seemed unlikely when you considered the frame of mind he was in—or something, someone had prevented his getting to Gordon.

Ford smiled at the lawman. 'Reckon it doesn't matter, Marshal,' he said. 'Guess I'll be heading back for Gordon's. Obliged to you for your hospitality.'

Dorsett managed a faint grin. 'You're welcome. Come again.'

Tom moved out into the warm sunlight. He heard Dorsett's voice from the doorway. 'Your horse is down at Richter's stable. Might as well take Witcher's with you, too. Belongs to JOG.'

Ford nodded, then slanted across the deserted street for the livery barn. He called for both mounts, and while they were being saddled, he went into a restaurant a few doors farther along and had two cups of coffee. He was not hungry and the strong, black liquid satisfied his needs completely—but did nothing to quiet the turmoil in his mind.

The feeling that something had happened to Gillen was a growing conviction—and, if so, the possibility of a range war was many times multiplied. The ranchers and homesteaders Gillen represented would accept it as a final straw in their struggle against Gordon, and whether they were correct or not in assuming the owner of JOG was behind their troubles, they would strike back.

Then would come the bloodshed and a lot of innocent people would get hurt—Susan Gordon for one, and his newly found friends Calico Jones and Cletus Todd, not to mention those unknown to him who would line up with the opposing faction. He gave little thought to Bill Tusas and the men who ran with him. They would take care of themselves, even enjoy such a blood letting; or perhaps they would pull out when the trouble started.

Maybe that was the wise thing for him to do—ride on before he became involved. He had been through range wars before, knew what they meant, had experienced the ruthless activities both sides could engage in. It was no pleasant memory.

After all, it was no business of his; he had been an employee of Jay Gordon's for only a day and two nights, if you counted from the beginning—and not a very welcome employee, at that, judging from Gordon's attitude. A smart man would move on, would shake the dust of the vengeance-threatened valley from his boots and get as far away as possible before all hell broke loose.

A smart man would do just that.

He guessed he wasn't very smart. He couldn't find it in himself to run, to dodge the impending bloodbath. Somehow he felt he had an obligation to someone, or something—he was not sure which—to stay in the valley and do all in his power to prevent the clash. It seemed to him he was standing in the middle, a solitary, lonely gun, and that only he knew the facts of the situation and was in a position to do something about them.

He was positive Jay Gordon was no land grabber, no seeker of limitless range; and he could understand how Gillen and the men lined up with him felt. The job was to make both sides see the truth, come to a meeting of minds and iron out their differences before it was too late.

How?

Ford sloshed the last of the coffee about in the cup, tipped it to his lips and drank it down. Start with Gillen, he thought. Find the rancher, if he was still alive, and take him to see Jay Gordon. Let him tell the owner of JOG his grievances. If Gordon denied any responsibility, they could then pool their efforts and get to the bottom of the problem. If Gordon admitted to the charges—well, then he would be faced with a decision; one that had to do with staying on or riding out.

Where would he find Gillen?

Tom considered that question as he returned to the stable. The horses were ready and after settling with the hostler for their keep with the last of his money, he mounted up and left the town.

Gillen was the key. Get him together with Jay Gordon. That was the one thought in his mind. Then he would know the straight of the matter. But where was Gillen? The question plagued him and lifted again a vague fear he had felt back in the jail at Prairie Grove. The rancher had never arrived at JOG. Why?

A short mile from the settlement Ford pulled to a halt. He had started back to Gordon's on the usual route, now a new thought occurred to him. He swung off the road abruptly, Witcher's horse trailing along at the end of the lead rope, and struck out across open country. He would locate the point where he had talked with Gillen and take up the rancher's trail from there. In so doing he should be able to learn what had happened.

He rode steadily and two hours later he reached the spot where he had halted to talk with the rancher. The hoof prints that led off to the east were not particularly distinct but they did form a trail and he set off at once.

They did not vary. Gillen had followed his directions exactly and the direct course he took was not that of a man considering a change of plan. The conviction that Gillen had run into trouble began to grow again and Ford found himself glancing anxiously ahead, hopeful of seeing some sign of the rancher, yet fearful that he might.

But the choppy hills and the shallow arroyos rolled on before him and he saw nothing but the gray, sparkling sand, the sun-dried grass and mesquite, and the shadowy shapes of smoke trees. Occasionally he frightened a jackrabbit into flight and once a flock of crested quail skittered out from under his pony's hoofs, but there was nothing more.

He dropped down into a long swale. Beyond its far ridge a column of smoke spiraled lazily into the steel blue of the sky. That would be the Gordon ranch. He was not many miles from it now. Another hour and he would be there. And if he found no sign of Gillen by then—what next?

He was pondering that when a dark blur lying to one side in the distance caught his eyes. He pulled to a halt and studied the object with narrow interest. It could be an out-cropping of rock, a thick stand of brush—or it could be something else. From where he sat he could not be sure of anything.

He swung off the tracks Gillen's horse had made, and angled toward the object. Best to make certain. As he drew closer he saw it was not a rocky ledge, as he had at first thought. A few minutes later he realized it was something besides weeds. The colors, while dusty, were not natural.

A short time after that he was near enough

to see cloth—clothing of some sort. It could be a cast off jacket, a shirt thrown aside by some rider. Or possibly it was a blanket.

And then Tom Ford stopped speculating. He saw a hat laying off to one side. He recognized a man's arm thrust out at a stiff angle, a leg doubled beneath a crumpled body. He spurred forward and dropped beside the lifeless shape. The man's back was up. A crusted, dark mass showed where a bullet had entered the body, just below the left shoulder.

Still hopeful, yet knowing whom he would find, Tom rolled the man over. It was Gillen.

CHAPTER TEN

Tom Ford rose quickly to his feet. He swung his glance about in a full circle. The killer, whoever he was, could yet be lurking in the area. But the hills and hollows into which he could see appeared deserted. There was no sign of Gillen's horse either, and Ford wondered about that.

He found the prints of the animal, saw where it had leaped forward when the bullet had struck the rancher. The horse had wheeled and Gillen had tumbled from its back and piled up against a clump of sawgrass. The drygulcher had evidently waited behind a low rise off the left, judging from the angle of the bullet. It was strange he had not been noticed by the rancher, Tom thought, and then he realized it would have been dark.

Satisfied that the killer no longer was nearby, Ford lifted the rancher's body and laid it across the saddle of Barney Witcher's horse. He anchored it securely with the same strip of rawhide they had used on the redhead. That done, Ford considered the best course to follow—return to Prairie Grove with Gillen's body, or continue on to Gordon's ranch.

He decided on the latter since it was much nearer, and he had a sudden urge to see what effect the body of Gillen would have on Jay Gordon when he beheld it. Often a great deal could be determined from a man's reaction to something unexpected.

He mounted up and rode on, his thoughts again deeply involved in the slowly but surely rising trouble that was enveloping the valley. There was something to Gillen's claim; that was certain now. And it was critical enough to cause the death of the rancher.

Tom Ford's thoughts came to a full stop on that; Gillen was kept from seeing Gordon. That could mean only one thing. Gordon was unaware of something that was taking place—something so important that Gillen was murdered before he could confront Jay Gordon with it.

Who could be involved? Mentally Tom Ford ticked off the few men he knew who worked for JOG; Calico Jones, Todd, other old timers on the ranch. It could scarcely be any of them. Quint Magee—possibly. Despite what Calico had said about the foreman, he was a good suspect. And then there were Tusas and his crowd; hardcases, killers if need be, but with hardly a reason.

Tusas was not likely one to be interested in operating a ranch of his own. Neither would Ben Poe or Sharpe or Hugh Chesser. They were the sort who lived for the excitement of living, who never wished to be tied down for long. No—Magee was the most likely prospect; Quint Magee with his quick, quiet ways, his over-subservience to Jay Gordon. He hoped the foreman would be on hand when he rode in with Gillen's body.

Ford was not disappointed.

When he turned into the yard through the high, square gate he saw Magee, with Calico Jones, come out of a shed and start toward the bunkhouse. They saw him at the same instant and halted. He rode on, pointing for the hitchrack in front of the main house.

As he halted at the rail the two men came trotting up. Jones walked to Witcher's horse and lifted the dead man's head. He looked closely, frowned, then glanced at Ford.

'Who's this?'

'Rancher named Gillen,' Tom replied, swinging down. 'Ever see him before?'

'Not me,' Calico said.

Ford's eyes were on Magee. 'How about you, Quint?' The foreman shook his head. 'Stranger to me. What happened? Where'd you find him?'

'West of here,' Tom answered. 'Gordon up and around?'

Magee nodded. 'In his office, or was a few minutes ago,' he said, then added. 'I'd steer clear of him for a spell, was I you. He's a little riled over Witcher.'

'This won't wait,' Tom said and started for the door.

At his knock the door opened immediately and Susan Gordon stood before him. She gave him a small smile and said, 'Yes?'

'Like to see your father.'

She hesitated. 'You're—you're the new man, Ford, aren't you? I don't know if it's wise—'

'It will be all right,' Tom said. 'And it's important.'

She stepped aside and he entered. He moved for the doorway that led into the rancher's office, hearing Jones and Quint Magee come in behind him. As he stepped into the room Jay Gordon glanced up from a newspaper. His eyes flared angrily when he saw Ford and he straightened in his chair.

'What the hell do you want?' he demanded.

'Brought a man to see you,' Tom replied coolly, watching the rancher closely. 'Only he's dead.'

'He's what?'

'Dead.'

Gordon's furious gaze swung to Magee. 'What's this all about, Quint?'

The foreman said, 'Don't know myself, Mr Gordon. He just now come riding in with a body across the saddle of Witcher's horse. Said he—'

'Man's name was Gillen,' Ford cut in. 'I found him drygulched about five miles west of here. Yesterday he told me he was on his way to see you.'

'Gillen?' Gordon repeated the name. 'Don't know anybody named Gillen. What did he want to see me about?'

'You sure you don't know?'

Gordon swore loudly. His face flushed angrily and he came from behind his desk with a few quick turns of his wheelchair.

'What do you mean by that, mister? Start talking sense or get the hell out of here! I don't know anybody called Gillen—dead or alive—and if I did, I'd say so. Who killed him? Sure it wasn't you?'

'Not me,' Tom said quietly, unmoved by the rancher's outburst. 'He was dead when I found him.'

'You said he told you he was coming to see me.'

'That was yesterday.'

'I recollect somethin',' Calico Jones said. 'The marshal was here last night. He was askin' around about somebody named Gillen.'

'What's it got to do with me?' Gordon shouted. 'You got a lot of guts, Ford, coming in here crawling me like I had something to do with a bushwhacking! You—a gunslinger who just shot down one of my hands, and maybe the one who murdered my boy.'

Tom Ford came to rigid attention. He stared at the rancher. In the sudden, tension filled hush he heard Quint Magee shift his feet, heard Calico Jones swallow hard. In one flashing instant of time he knew what had been on Jay Gordon's mind, understood his peculiar actions in hiring him, the meaning of the questions he had asked. Gordon believed, for some reason, that he had been the man who had shot down Jock, his son. The rancher had put him to work as a means for keeping him around until he could check, be sure before he exacted his vengeance.

'I'm not the man who gunned down your son,' he said, finding his voice. 'You're wrong, Gordon.'

'His name was Ford!' the rancher said. It was plain he had spoken without thinking, that he had tipped his hand before he was ready. Now he was making the best of it. 'You fit. You've got the name and you're too damned handy with that iron you carry. You killed Witcher—drew and hit him dead center with him standing there already holding a gun in his hand they say—and now you come stomping in here with a wild bull yarn about finding a dead man.'

His name was Ford!

Tom was hearing that over and over in his mind. *His name was Ford!* Inwardly he was trembling. It had been Fresno. It had been his own brother who killed Jock Gordon. It could have been no one else.

'You heard me? You're a murdering, sneaking gunslinger! You're going—'

Ford became conscious of Gordon's seething words. He moved a step nearer the rancher and faced him squarely. 'I shot Witcher. I admit it. He gave me no choice. But I didn't kill your son, or this man Gillen. That's the truth whether you believe it or not.'

'Didn't expect you to admit it,' Gordon said. 'But I go by the looks of things. It's all mighty pat—so pat there's no doubt in my mind. I'd figured to keep you around until I could check back and find out a few things for sure. Far as I'm concerned it's not necessary now. First Witcher, then this Gillen. Before that maybe a dozen more—including my boy.'

'Jay, you got Tom plumb wrong!' Calico Jones broke in. 'I know he didn't—'

'You don't know any more about him than I do!' Gordon snapped. 'Quint, get a couple of the boys and take him in to Dorsett. Tell Art I want him locked up. I'll be in and file murder charges against him. Then I want you to take off for Colorado, see if you can round up any witnesses to Jock's killing. Understand—'

'Yes, sir, Mr Gordon—'

'Hold on a minute!' Tom Ford's voice cracked like a whip in the small room. 'You can't prove anything like that because I had nothing to do with it.'

'Then you got no worrying to do,' Gordon said. 'But I figure you have. You're my man, sure enough, and I've been looking for the day when I could stand by and watch you swing.'

'Listen to me, Gordon! I'm trying to do you a favor. This man Gillen was a rancher. He was coming here to see you, to warn you that you've got a range war on your hands if you don't call off the raids you've been pulling.'

'Range war! Raids! What kind of a dodge you trying to pull now? I'm beginning to think you're plain loco! Get him out of here, Quint!'

'You're a damn fool—' Tom began and went silent as he felt the hard, round muzzle of Magee's pistol jam into his spine.

'All right, Ford,' the foreman murmured. 'Just take it easy. Raise your hands, slow.'

A wild burst of anger and frustration rocked through Tom. There was no talking to Gordon, no reasoning with him. It was useless to try and make him see he was wrong, that he was in danger. Hate so clouded his mind he could think of nothing else. But the matter had gone far enough and was getting out of hand. He must act, or it would be too late.

Lifting his arms, he wheeled slowly about. Calico Jones, his long face screwed into deep set lines of worry, stood against the wall. Quint Magee, his eyes cool, met his own gaze.

'No cute tricks now, Ford.'

'Sure,' Tom said and lashed out with his hand.

He knocked the gun from the foreman's grasp, sending it skating across the floor to Calico's feet. He leaped for the door, drawing his own weapon. Gordon yelled something and Magee, lunging, closed in fast. Tom whirled and drove his fist into the foreman's jaw; it sent him reeling into Jones.

Ford raced into the adjoining parlor. Susan, apparently in there since the start of things, stared at him with a white, strained face. He ducked his head at her.

'Sorry,' he muttered and plunged through

the doorway onto the porch.

He reached the hitchrack in a half-a-dozen long strides. He reached for the reins of the black and jerked them free. Gordon was shouting inside the house and back somewhere close to the barn Tom could hear boots pounding across the hard pack. He wasted no time looking, but vaulted onto the saddle and spun the pony about, spurring it into a gallop. He was just passing beneath the arch of the gate when the first gunshot echoed across the morning air, and he knew the chase was on.

CHAPTER ELEVEN

Tom pulled away rapidly. For the first quarter mile nothing but flat, open land rolled out before him, offering no cover of any sort. Then to the left he saw a dark band; a brushy arroyo or perhaps a narrow grove of stunted trees, he could not tell which. Immediately he began to swerve the wiry little black for it.

He wished that he had his own buckskin. He would have felt better, had more confidence if he were astride a horse he knew well. But he could not complain about the cow pony he was riding. It had responded to his every demand, and while he knew it would need rest soon, it was showing no reluctance to run.

Ford glanced over his shoulder. Three riders were pouring through the gate. They were too distant to identify accurately. One was Quint Magee, he was certain of that. Another appeared to be Calico Jones. The third was not familiar. He could make out the figure of Jay Gordon, in his wheelchair, on the gallery. Susan stood nearby. It was not difficult to imagine the temper the contentious old rancher would be in at that moment and he could not help feeling sorry for the girl.

He drew closer to the smudge of dark color and saw that it was a narrow, overgrown arroyo slashing its path across the prairie. It bore toward the mountains in the distance, apparently serving as one of the innumerable drains for carrying off the spring thaws and summer rains.

He reached it, swung down onto the sandy floor, and raced on. Magee and the others would have seen him duck into the brush, and he could not expect to shake them by that particular maneuver. They would follow, but it did remove him from their sight and that afforded possibilities.

Magee would expect him to continue in flight along the ravine with the mountains as his ultimate goal. The foreman would bend his efforts toward overtaking him before he could gain the safety of the wooded slopes. He must permit Magee to believe that—and find some other route for escape.

His eyes searched ahead. A ragged shoulder of rock jutting out into the arroyo, almost blocking it, came into view. Hope lifted within Tom Ford and he rushed toward it. But it offered no sanctuary. Its farther side proved to be a steep, shale covered slope devoid of brush.

He hurried on, feeling the black beginning to tire now as the grade and loose sand took their toll of the horse's strength. A thickening of brush appeared. Again Ford's hopes rose. He drew abreast of the tangled mass of greasewood, cacti, brier and doveweed and saw that it was the mouth of a narrow, feeder arroyo cutting in at right angles. Without hesitation he swung into it.

He spurred the heaving cowpony on for a dozen yards and then halted behind a screening bulge of rock. He dropped from the saddle and trotted back to the main ravine. He ripped a branch from a nearby bush and quickly erased the hoof prints in the loose sand where he had turned off. Those on the floor he ignored; the tracks of other riders before him were plentiful enough to cover his retreat. Finished, he returned to where his horse waited.

Magee and his men were not long in coming. They had pulled up rapidly. Ford watched the foreman ride by. He was bent forward on his saddle, his eyes intent on the brush ahead. Close behind came the second rider, one Tom had not met. Calico Jones, a dozen paces to his rear, came last. The old puncher's gaze was on the floor of the arroyo. He was not trusting blindly to the supposition that Ford would continue on to the mountains.

Ford allowed the men to pass. He must give them time to get beyond both sight and hearing distance before he pulled out. There was little cover elsewhere in which he could hide if he moved too soon, and they saw him.

He waited five long minutes and then rose and stepped to the saddle. He reached for the leathers—and then froze. The unmistakable sound of a horse walking slowly on the sand came to him. Quick alarm rushed through Tom Ford. He had held off too long. Magee had not fallen for the ruse and was doubling back. His hand dropped to the gun at his hip. He didn't want to shoot it out with the foreman, or any of the men, but he was not going back to a cell in Prairie Grove—not until he got a few things straightened out.

'Tom?'

It was Calico Jones. Still unsure, Ford remained quiet, riding out the moments. He didn't think the old rider would trick him but he could take no chances.

'Tom? It's me—Calico. Others've gone on. Seen you'd cut off the trail but I didn't say nothin'. You up there in the rocks?'

'Here,' Ford answered, the tautness leaving his rigid frame. 'Up the draw.'

He wheeled the black around and walked him quietly down to the floor of the arroyo. Jones watched in silence.

'Expect we'd better get out of here,' Ford said as he drew alongside the old man. 'Quint could turn back.'

Jones shook his head. 'Ain't likely. He's dead certain you're leggin' it for the mountains. He won't quit 'til he gets there. What's this all about, anyway?'

'Not sure myself,' Tom said, reaching for his cigarette makings. 'What I said to Gordon was the truth—about myself and about Gillen.'

'This Gillen—he really comin' to talk range war to Jay?'

'Yes. When I ran into him late yesterday he was all worked up over it. Claims Gordon, or men working for him, have been raiding the ranchers and homesteaders over in a valley west of here, forcing them to sell out.'

'He's plumb loco,' Jones said flatly. 'Jay ain't up to no such thing. I'd swear to it.'

'What I told Gillen, but he claimed he had proof. And maybe he has.'

Calico frowned and tugged at his chin.

'How you figure that?'

'Somebody sure didn't want Gillen talking to Gordon. Bushwhacked him before he got the chance.'

'That's right,' the old puncher said. 'But who?'

'How about Quint Magee?'

Calico was startled. 'Him? What makes you think he'd be mixed up in somethin' like that? And what for?'

'Don't know but there's something about him I can't figure out. And he seems the most likely one.'

'You're sayin' you think somebody, maybe Quint, is pullin' off these here raids and blamin' it on to Gordon?'

'Assuming it isn't Gordon, that's the way it looks to me.'

'Why? What for?'

'Who knows? Maybe he wants the land. Maybe something is going to happen—like a railroad coming through that nobody else has heard about. Maybe he just wants to build himself a ranch. Could be several reasons.'

Calico wagged his grizzled head doubtfully. 'Sure don't sound much like Quint to me. He's too wound up in JOG to think of much else.'

'Could just want everybody to think that.'

'Sure, could be. What about this other thing that's stickin' in Jay's craw—your bein' the man that gunned down his boy?'

'Wasn't me, Calico. You've got my word on that.'

'What I thought. You got any feelings about who it was?'

Tom said, 'Yes,' and dropped the subject there. 'I'm riding on west, over to that valley where Gillen lives. Seems to me that's the best place to start getting to the bottom of things.'

'Makes sense,' Calico agreed. 'You mind a little company?'

'Be glad to have you,' Tom replied. He looked back up the arroyo. 'Feel better after we've put some distance between Magee and us. Just as soon not run up against him until I know for sure about things. You know where Gillen's place would be?'

Jones said, 'Nope, but I reckon it won't be no big chore findin' out. You said it was in a valley west of here. Put him near the county line. Jay's land runs up mighty close to the edge. Expect Gillen and the rest will be right in there somewhere.'

'Let's move out then,' Ford said, touching his pony lightly with his spurs. 'Can't get there any too soon.'

Jones swung in beside Ford and together they doubled back along the arroyo until they reached a gentle slope that permitted them to climb out onto level ground once more. There the old puncher halted and threw his gaze out across the land.

'Reckon we'd better keep to the north,' he said, 'unless we want to run smack into Bill Tusas and his bunch. They're with the herd. Bill's been doin' a powerful lot of talkin' about how he's goin' to meet up with you and square things for Witcher.'

'He had his time, and didn't take it,' Ford murmured.

'Claims you had the drop on him and would've shot him down cold like you did Barney, if he'd made a move. Says all he wants is a chance to fair draw you in a stand-up shoot-out.'

Ford sighed. 'Way things are shaping up around here,' he said wearily, 'looks like he'll have to get in line and wait his turn.'

CHAPTER TWELVE

They pushed their horses, and late that afternoon, with the slanting sunlight hot on their faces, they reached a low run of black rock buttes that marked the western boundary of Jay Gordon's vast JOG spread.

'Reckon we're there,' Calico Jones said as they halted to breathe their mounts. 'Gillen's and them other places ought to be from here on.'

'Nothing in sight,' Ford replied, looking

off across the flats. To their right, ten miles or so distant, the first uplifting of the mountains began. Ahead and to the left there was only the rolling swells and dips of the prairie country.

'Heard tell there's a fair size river around somewheres,' Jones said, shifting to a more comfortable position on his saddle. 'My hunch is we'll find the houses close to it?'

'Where's Rock Springs from here? Gillen said they did their trading there.'

'A far piece south,' Calico replied. 'We goin' to it?'

Ford shook his head. 'No need. Just wondered. We ought to find what we're looking for around the ranches and farms.'

They resumed their journey, again pointing directly into the sun. An hour later they stopped on the lip of a long, low escarpment. Below them a broad and lengthy valley spread in a panorama of varying greens and browns. Here and there patches of vivid wild flowers broke the sameness, and on its yonder side the bright glitter of water marked the course of a stream.

Immediately ahead of them they saw the blackened, charred remains of what had been a small house.

'We found it, I reckon,' Calico said laconically. 'Mighty pretty country. Sure can see why somebody's wantin' it so bad.'

They rode off the ledge through a brushy gap and came into the ruined farm from its back side. Halting in the center of the yard they looked about. It had been a small house, probably of two rooms, and it had been constructed entirely of wood. A battered cook stove canted drunkenly on three legs in one corner. In the opposite corner lay the remains of an iron-bound trunk. There had been three smaller outbuildings and apparently no barn. Posts forming a corral had been uprooted and, together with the connecting rails, had been dragged into a pile where a torch had been applied. Whoever had captained the raid had done a thorough job.

'Gillen wasn't lying,' Tom Ford murmured.

'That's for sure,' Jones said. 'What's next? Sure ain't nobody left around here we can talk to about it.'

'Keep riding,' the tall cowboy said. 'Bound to run into somebody eventually.'

Two miles farther along they found a second homestead. It, too, had been burned to ashes. The third, considerably larger than the first two, was near the river. The fly-blown carcasses of a horse and two milk cows lay shriveling in the sunlight just behind what had been a barn. A well-house had been tipped over and the remains of another horse had been dumped into the shaft, where it was wedged part way down.

'Somebody wants this valley mighty bad,' Jones said, wrinkling his nose at the rank odor. 'And they ain't stoppin' at nothin' to get it.'

The pattern was clear. The raiders had started at the upper reaches of the vast swale and were working southward. It was not difficult to understand the agitation that gripped those who lived in the lower end.

'Wonder where we'll find Gillen's place,' Ford said, that thought bringing to mind the necessity for performing a disagreeable chore. 'Ought to tell his people what happened to him.'

'Could be a ticklish job,' Jones said.

'Looks like we're the only ones in a position to do it.'

'Sure, you're right. Expect if we keep ridin' we'll run into somebody who can tell us—unless whoever is up to this devilment has done cleaned out the whole valley.'

'Looks like a house over there at the foot of those buttes,' Tom said suddenly, pointing toward the southeast. 'Let's try it.'

'At least it ain't been burned to the ground,' Calico said as they continued on.

The place—a single room shack, a corral, and a small feed and tool shed—was deserted. There was no evidence of fire, of a struggle or anything out of the ordinary. It was as if the owner had simply walked off taking only personal belongings and abandoning all else.

It was not hard to figure. Where the three settlers to the north had resisted and brought the fiery wrath of the raiders down upon their heads, this man, apparently a small rancher, had quickly acceded to their threats and demands, and had pulled out. Perhaps he had received some token payment, or possibly fear alone had done the job. Regardless, the place was dead—as dead as its fire-ravaged neighbors.

They rode on keeping within sight of the river, knowing that all the homesteaders and ranchers would have built in its vicinity. The sun was swinging lower and Tom Ford realized they must soon find an inhabited dwelling or else delay until the following day to pursue their quest.

'Smoke up ahead,' Calico announced.

Ford threw his glance to the direction in which the old puncher pointed. It was a small column, he saw, and one that would be rising from a chimney not from a raid. They spurred their tired horses to a lope and soon reached the house. It was a small, clapboard affair placed at the rear of a field in which a good stand of corn flourished. As they turned into the lane that led between two fences, a man came from a shed to meet them. A woman appeared a moment later, halting in the doorway of the main house.

She watched them suspiciously.

They drew to a stop in front of the man, a squat, redfaced individual in faded, patched overalls and thick-soled, knobby-toed work shoes.

'Howdy,' Ford greeted him.

The man nodded in sullen silence. Somewhere a door slammed. 'What do you want?' he demanded finally in a hostile voice.

'Looking for the Gillen place,' Calico answered. 'This happen to be it?'

The man shook his head. 'Why would you be huntin' him?'

'Not hunting him,' Tom said. 'Just want to talk to his people. Know where he lives?'

'Maybe.'

Ford stared at the homesteader, impatience and vague anger stirring him. 'Well?'

'On south—about three miles.'

'Much obliged,' Ford said. 'Looks like you've been having some trouble,' he added. 'Saw some places that have been burned down.'

'Reckon you ought to know,' the farmer snapped and wheeled about abruptly.

Calico watched the man stalk off thoughtfully. 'Sure is an unfriendly sort of cuss,' he observed drily.

Tom pulled the black around to the lane. 'Guess any man would be, considering what's happening here in this valley. Let's get on to Gillen's before dark.'

They returned to the faintly marked road and cut to their right. The Gillen ranch, a two-storied affair with several good outbuildings and corrals came into sight a short time later. The place was set on a low hill, slightly above the surrounding terrain, and overlooked the country for a considerable distance. Gillen had planted cottonwoods along three sides and a ditch, running full with sparkling water and curved off from the river, made a looping journey to the garden growing just beyond the structures.

'Sure can't blame a man for fightin' for a place like that,' Calico said as they rode into the yard.

Tom nodded. His eyes were on the house. He could see someone standing in the doorway and a white face peered out from one of the upper floor windows. There were three horses tied to the hitch rack at the side and a buckboard had been halted near the barn.

'Sure looks quiet,' Calico muttered. 'Can't say as I like the smell of things.'

'Woman there at the door,' Tom said. 'Must be some men around ... Those horses and that buckboard...'

'More horses around back,' the old puncher said. 'Got a feelin' we're ridin' into somethin', Tom.'

'Maybe so. Not much chance to back out now. Keep behind me a little. Watch sharp.'

Jones, reining in his mount, held off for a few moments and allowed Ford to pull away. Then he resumed, advancing slow and wary.

They reached the broad, hard-packed area of the yard that separated the house from the barn. Tom saw the horses Calico had noted then; six more, all saddled and standing near a pole corral. He glanced toward the house. The woman no longer stood in the doorway. He could not see the upper window, his view now shut off by the corner of the building. He came to the center of the yard and stopped.

'Hello—the house?' he called.

A dog, somewhere inside, began to bark, and in the barn a door creaked loudly.

'Anybody home?'

The back screen swung open. A short, heavy woman in a long housedress and wearing an apron appeared. Placing her hands on her hips, she stared at Ford.

'What do you want?' she asked in a harsh tone.

'You Mrs Gillen?'

'No. She's inside. What do you want?'

'Like to talk to her.'

'Reckon you'd better do your talking to us,' a man's deep voice, coming from the barn, broke in. 'Now, don't either of you make a move. There's seven guns laid down on you and we'd as soon blast you off them horses as draw a breath!'

CHAPTER THIRTEEN

Tom Ford sat motionless on his saddle. A cold prickle raced up his spine. He heard Calico Jones mutter something under his breath and then the sound of slow, cautious footsteps reached him.

'Don't get betwixt them and the guns!' a voice warned.

A moment later Tom felt his pistol being lifted from its holster. He heard Jones mutter again and knew he also had been relieved of his weapon.

'Now step down—both of you,' the same voice commanded. 'And don't try running. You'd not get six feet.'

Someone laughed loudly. 'That's just what they're goin' to get—six feet—of ground!'

Ford dismounted carefully, then came slowly around to face his captors. There were ten of them. Nine were dressed in the usual rough work garb of ranchers and farmers. The tenth wore a neat gabardine suit, a white shirt complete with string tie and a soft, gray hat. He was a slight, wiry man, somewhere in his late forties, with a sharp face and small, faded blue eyes that were almost colorless.

'What's this all about?' Ford asked, looking squarely at the man. 'We're here as friends.'

'Friends!' a voice in the crowd snarled. 'Tell them, Henry! Tell them what it's all about!'

The well-dressed man holstered his pistol and took a step nearer Tom and Calico Jones. Leaning forward, he peered closely at them.

'Which one of you murdered Herb Gillen?'

Ford started visibly. Jones swore. A man in the front said, 'Surprised you, eh? Didn't know we'd found out about it already.'

'Never mind, Claude,' the well-dressed one said. 'Let me handle it.'

'Sure, Mr Stalcup, sure.'

'We know about Gillen,' Stalcup said, clasping his hands together. 'His horse started back for home after Herb was killed. George Manson, there, found the animal in his field. There was blood on the saddle. He is dead isn't he?'

Tom nodded. 'I found him.'

'Where is the body?'

'I took it to the Gordon ranch.'

A growl went up from the men. One surged forward. 'Might of knowed that's what they'd do! Kill him, then take him to their ranch for everybody to gape and gander at.'

'All right, Bert,' Stalcup said, motioning the homesteader back into the ranks. 'You've asked me to be your spokesman. Let me do things my way.'

The angry grumbling died off. Stalcup faced Ford and Calico Jones again. 'We've been expecting you. We figured that after Gillen's horse showed up this morning, you'd be back in the valley tonight. Reason we're all together and waiting. We thought there would be more. Where's the rest of your party?'

'There's nobody but us,' Tom answered. Sweat had begun to stand on his forehead in small beads. Stalcup was a strange one. He had a quiet, firm way of talking that set Ford's nerves on edge. 'If you'll give me a chance to speak.'

'Did Herb Gillen get to talk to your boss, to Jay Gordon?' Stalcup cut in icily, paying no attention at all to Ford.

'No. He was ambushed before he reached the ranch.'

Henry Stalcup lifted his arms, then let them fall in a gesture of helplessness. 'You see?' he said, turning to the homesteaders. 'You see what kind of a man this Gordon is? Poor Herb died for nothing. He didn't even set foot on the Gordon ranch. He was killed before he got there.'

Again the crowd pushed forward angrily. 'String 'em up!' someone cried. 'Ain't no sense in all this yammerin'. Let's get it over with and head for Gordon's!'

Stalcup waved his hands for silence. He wheeled back around to Tom and Calico. 'We had hoped to avoid trouble but Gordon leaves us no choice. We're determined to stop his raiding and burning. We're moving in on him and handing him some of his own medicine!'

'Wait!' Ford shouted and took a step forward, ignoring the array of shotguns and rifles leveled at him. 'You've got this all wrong. That's the reason we're here. We're not raiders.'

'You're forkin' horses that're wearin' Gordon's brand, ain't you?' the man called Claude demanded.

'Yes, but we—'

'And you ride for Gordon—and do what he tells you to, don't you?'

'Gordon's not raiding your places!' Ford yelled, drowning out Claude's voice. 'He doesn't want your land, never has far as I know.'

'Then who is it?' Stalcup asked. 'And how does it happen they ride horses with the JOG brand—just like you're on?'

'I don't know. That's what we're trying to find out. We rode over here—'

'Gordon send you?'

'No. We came on our own. Wanted to tell Gillen's family what had happened to him and see if we couldn't get to the bottom of things before a range war started.'

'It's started, sure as hell,' Claude declared, wagging his head. 'And you ain't foolin' us one whit! I'll bet the rest of your bunch is somewhere in the valley right now, burnin' and shootin' and maybe killin' some poor devil.'

'You ever see one of these raiders up close?' Tom rushed on, ignoring the man. 'Close enough to get a good look at him, I mean.'

'How could we? They're wearin' black masks or toe sacks over their heads How we goin' to see what they look like? All we can go by is their horses. They always ride Gordon's stock. That's how we know who's behind it.'

'I tell you he's not behind it!' Ford shouted. 'He doesn't know a damn thing about it!'

'Who you trying to fool?' Stalcup asked quietly. 'Would you like to see proof? We can show you the hide of one of the horses Bert Fallon shot when they raided his place. It's nailed there to the barn.'

'I know about that. Gillen told me.'

A sudden hush dropped over the men. Stalcup looked keenly at Ford. 'You talked to Herb?'

Tom nodded. 'Met him yesterday on my way to town. Said he was heading out to Gordon's, wanted to talk things over, warn him about the trouble that was coming.'

'And you found his body, too, you said?'

'I did. That was this morning.'

Stalcup leaned forward. 'You wouldn't know just how he was killed, would you?'

'Shot in the back, with a rifle, I'd guess. When I found him—'

Stalcup had turned away. 'I'd say we've discovered the very man that murdered Herb Gillen,' he said, facing the crowd. 'Admits he met him yesterday, that he was the one who picked up the body and carried it in to Gordon's ranch. Also, he knows how it was done—a rifle bullet in the back.'

A yell went up. Ford glanced at Calico Jones and swore in helpless fury. Stalcup was a smooth talker with the knack of making things said come out different. And he held the homesteaders and ranchers in the palm of his hand. He could make them see and believe anything he wished.

Ford took a firm grasp of his nerves and his temper. He and the old puncher were in a tight spot, and unless he remained calm and made Stalcup and the others see reason, it could cost them their lives. He reached out and took Stalcup by the arm to draw his attention.

'Not the way of it at all,' he said. 'I don't

know who killed Gillen. I'm no more guilty of that than Gordon is of pulling those raids.'

'Hard to believe,' Stalcup replied. 'How do you explain the fact the raiders ride JOG horses?'

'I can't,' Ford said, shaking his head. 'Maybe they stole the stock ... Maybe they've got one of Gordon's branding irons, or made one like it. I don't know—but you can believe this; Gordon isn't who you want and if you raid his place, you'll start something that will never end until he's run down every last one of you.'

'If he's able,' Claude said quietly. 'We figure to do the job up right. Time we're done there won't be nobody left to do nothin'.'

'You're a bunch of fools!' Tom exclaimed in exasperation, forgetting his determination to remain calm. 'Use your heads! You think we would have ridden in here like we did if things were the way you claim?'

'That doesn't mean anything,' Stalcup said, taking charge again. 'I expect you and your friend there came on ahead just to look things over at the Gillen place—get all set before the rest of your bunch showed up. Only it misfired. You didn't expect Herb's horse to wander home and tip us off.'

'We came here to tell Mrs Gillen what had happened to her husband,' Tom repeated stubbornly. 'And to see if we could find out something about—'

'Sure, sure,' the man named Bert said, breaking in. 'You're a right kind-hearted pair of critters. Only thing, while one of you was talkin' to Gillen's woman, the other one would be fixin' it so's the rest of your renegades could slip in easy and take over.'

'Ain't no use talkin', Tom,' Calico Jones said, speaking for the first time. 'They ain't about to listen to what you've got to say.'

'You can bet on it!' Stalcup snapped. 'We're not swallowing any such cock and bull yarn—and it's time we stopped listening and did something. I first thought we should take you two down to Rock Springs and turn you over to the marshal for a trial. Now I'm not so sure it would be smart. If the rest of your gang is somewhere in the valley, we'd be playing right into their hands. Don't think we ought to leave.'

'Why bother with them? String them up—that's the answer!'

Stalcup stared thoughtfully at the speaker. 'No doubt you're right, but we can't do it here in front of the women folk. Ought to wait until we can take them out where they'll be found by their own bunch.'

'What difference will that make?' Claude asked. 'This time tomorrow there won't be no Gordon ranch left, anyway!'

'We may have to hold up the raid for another day,' Stalcup said, glancing toward

the sun, just dropping below the horizon.
'We need more men.'

'There's enough. Be twelve all told when the others get here.'

'Take more than that. You've got to remember Gordon's got hardcases, outlaws and gunslingers working for him. They're used to something like this. Can't afford to underestimate them.'

'What you can't afford,' Tom said pointedly, 'is to go ahead with what you're planning. It'll be the start of the bloodiest range war the country ever saw.'

'That's for certain!' Calico added, warmly. 'Don't you fellers think for a minute you're up against a greenhorn when you take on Jay Gordon! He was out here fightin' Injuns, renegades, rustlers, the weather and everythin' else for his piece of the land long before most of you ever knowed it was here. And he might be crippled up some now, but he's still a better man than any of you—and he'll take you on—'

Claude lunged forward and struck out at Jones. The old puncher took the blow in his belly, gasped and sagged to his knees. The homesteader drew back his fist for a second blow. Ford, suddenly seeing red, leaped in between the two men. Catching Claude by the shoulder, Tom spun him about. His right fist smashed into the homesteader's jaw, and sent him reeling back into the shadows.

Then something solid and swift descended upon Tom Ford's head and he was smothered by darkness.

CHAPTER FOURTEEN

Tom Ford opened his eyes slowly, an inborn caution keeping him entirely still until he became fully conscious and aware of the moment. A dull pain thudded inside his head, and his leg, where Barney Witcher's bullet had creased the flesh, was stinging. He was laying on a mound of straw, apparently in the barn, in one of the stalls. He could hear voices and the flickering reflection of a fire somewhere near the doorway danced on the ceiling and walls of the structure.

He felt someone move and realized it would be Calico Jones. He rolled over, fighting back a wave of nausea the sudden motion evoked, and looked at the old puncher. Jones was sitting up, hunched forward with his hands pressed against his belly.

'You all right?' Tom asked in a low, anxious whisper.

Calico's head swiveled around. In the half darkness Ford saw a grin crack his weathered face. 'Sure. How about you? Had me worried some.'

Tom sat up, moving carefully. He felt the back of his head gingerly, then groaned. 'Must have hit me with a pistol butt,' he muttered. 'What's been going on?'

'Not much. After they knocked you out they drug us in here. Seems they decided to hold off the raid until tomorrow. That feller Stalcup wants more men in on it.'

'What about us?'

'We're sure in a bucket full of trouble,' Calico replied, shaking his head soberly. 'Come daylight we're goin' to be the big attraction at a necktie party. Heard Stalcup say we was to be made an example of for anybody else who got the idea they could raid the valley.'

Ford's eyes narrowed. 'Long time until daylight,' he said, glancing toward the front of the barn. 'Any idea how many men they got watching over us?'

'Heard some of them ride out. Reckon there's six, maybe seven left. Don't see how we can get by them, howsomever.'

'Neither do I but we've got to figure a way. I'm not anxious to have my neck stretched—and Gordon's got to be warned.'

'For sure,' Calico said. 'You call the shots. I'll back your hand.'

'First thing to do is take a look around,' Tom said. 'Wait here.'

He crawled out of the stall, ignoring the throbbing in his head, and moved toward the front of the building. The compartments adjoining the one into which he and Calico had been thrown were empty, and for that he was grateful. He need not worry about frightening any horses and setting up a disturbance that would bring the homesteaders in at a run.

He worked his way to a window, raised himself cautiously and examined it. Spikes held it rigidly in place. It was not intended for ventilation, having been installed only for light. The others would be the same. He sank back on the dusty floor, then made a hurried circuit of the barn hoping for a second door. There was none. He paused, then glanced upward. Disappointment slogged through him again. There was no loft, only a shelf-like arrangement at one end upon which a few items had been stored. They were trapped in a cell as effective as one inside a jail.

Ford hunched up against a wall to think. The steady passage of time pushed at him, turning him tense and edgy. There had to be a way out—there must be. He could not sit back and wait and hope for something to happen. He had to find an answer. He glanced toward the door. Perhaps, if he moved in close, an idea might come to him.

On hands and knees, keeping well in the shadows, he made his way toward the wide entrance. Drawing close, he hunched below a line of harnesses hanging from pegs on the wall. The fire, unnecessary for warmth as the night was pleasant, had been built a dozen paces in front of the opening. Its glow lit up the surrounding area effectively.

There were five men standing about the flames. One was Claude, the others he did not know by name but they also had been in the original group. Henry Stalcup was not present.

'...Ought to be some way we can get them deeds back,' Claude was saying. 'If somethin' happens to Gordon, how'll we claim the land again?'

'He didn't get no deed from Agnew,' another man pointed out. 'Joe just picked up and left. Said if he couldn't have the place, nobody else could either.'

'He's the only one. Rest of them all signed over their property. Janowitz got a hundred dollars for his place. Reckon Gordon paid about the same for the others.'

'Won't make no difference to him whether he's got a deed or not,' Claude said. 'He'll just take over the place. Owning all the land around it, he might as well have the papers to it.'

'Maybe we ought to get Stalcup to talk to Gordon first, see if there's some way we can get them deeds.'

'Now, how you goin' to do that? Just have Henry walk up to him and say, "We're goin' to raid your place, burn it to the ground and shoot your head off, so how about handin' over the deeds to the thirty thousand acres of land you stole from us before we get started?" That it? Talk sense, Hobe!'

'Well, I just thought.'

'Stalcup ought to have an answer to it, bein' a lawyer,' Claude commented. 'When he shows up in the mornin' let's ask him about it.'

The homesteader moved back a few steps, picked up a handful of dry sticks and tossed them into the fire. 'Somebody better take a look at them prisoners.'

One of the men laughed. 'Why? They ain't gettin' out of there.'

'Sure. I know that but we ought to keep an eye on them. Stalcup said—'

Tom waited to hear no more. He dropped back into the darkness and hurried to the stall where Calico Jones waited. The old puncher greeted him eagerly.

'You figure a way—'

'Later,' Ford whispered. 'They're coming. Make out like you're asleep.'

Claude and two others appeared after a few moments. Dark, indefinite shapes, they loomed up at the end of the stall. Through half-shut eyelids Tom could see the glitter of guns held ready in their hands. There would be no opportunity for jumping them.

'Beats me how them two can sleep like

that,' one of the trio muttered. 'Was it me, I'd be wide awake, worryin' myself sick.'

'You ain't no outlaw,' Claude replied. 'You got a conscience, they ain't.'

They wheeled about, walked down the runway and resumed their places around the fire. Ford and Calico sat up.

'You find a way out of here?' Jones asked, renewing his question.

'Only one—out that front door,' Tom answered. 'It's the only way.'

'How about the windows?'

'They don't open. And there's no other door.'

Calico grunted. 'Ain't goin' to be easy.'

'Maybe,' Tom said as an idea began to build in his mind. 'Just maybe we've got a chance!'

He thrust a hand into the side pocket of his Levis and sighed in relief. He still had matches. Stalcup's men had relieved him of his gun belt but had taken nothing else. He held up a match for Jones to see. 'Fire—that's our ticket out of here,' he said softly.

'Fire?' Calico echoed blankly.

Ford nodded. 'Now listen. Crawl over to the far side of the door. You'll find a lot of harnesses and other gear hanging on the wall. Hunker down there and wait for me.'

'What're you figurin' to do?'

'Start a blaze in the straw. That ought to

bring them in fast.'

'And when they do we'll make it to the horses.'

'Right, only we'll have to slow them down some.'

'How?'

'Show you after we get set. Move out and be careful. Don't let them see you.'

Calico was already slipping away from the stall. Tom, tension mounting within him now, watched the dark blur that was the old rider cross the width of the barn, disappear briefly, and then reappear near the door. Ford began to rake some of the straw into a pile in the far corner of the stall. He must arrange it so he would have time to rejoin Calico before Claude and the others noted the flames. The fire, once started, would spread fast.

Satisfied with his preparations, he moved to a position where his body would hide the glare, and struck the match. He allowed it to burn for a moment, then placed it in the hollow he had created beneath the mound of dry stalks. It caught instantly. He whirled away and swiftly and silently ran to where Jones was crouched.

'It started?' Calico asked in a husky whisper.

'Going good,' Tom replied, looking toward the door.

'Now what?'

'The harnesses,' Ford said, reaching up and unhooking an arm load of the leather straps. 'When they come running in and start down the runway, throw it on them—tangle them up plenty.'

Calico Jones grinned his appreciation. 'Ought to do the job. They'll be in a powerful big hurry to get to the fire and if we mess them up with a lot of ropes and straps—'

A shout lifted in the yard. A voice cried, 'There's somethin' burnin' in the barn!'

'Get ready,' Tom murmured his warning. 'Here they come!'

All five of the homesteaders and ranchers appeared in the doorway suddenly. 'It's over there—in the stall!' Claude yelled. 'Get to it—quick. Stomp it out. I'll watch so's the prisoners don't make a break.'

'Goin' to need water—'

'Now!' Tom whispered and leaped to his feet.

He threw his arm load of harness at the four men wheeling into the runway. Behind him he heard Calico move and add his tangle of leather to the sudden confusion. A yell and a burst of cursing went up.

Ford saw Claude wheel. He lunged at the man. The rifle in Claude's hands blasted and Tom felt the hot breath of a bullet along his neck. In the next instant he was upon the man, dragging him to the floor. He smashed a balled fist into Claude's face, then felt him wilt and go limp.

He wrenched the rifle from the homesteader's hands and leaped to his feet. Calico was plunging through the doorway. The four other men were scrambling about in the shadowy depths of the barn, struggling to free themselves, and beyond them the fire in the stall was gaining rapidly.

Ford rushed out into the open. Calico Jones was a long step ahead of him. He did not know where the horses had been taken, but assumed they had been put with those he had seen at the hitchrack. They reached the center of the yard. He saw the horses then.

'This way!' he shouted at Jones.

They legged it across the hard pack and found their mounts. They jerked the reins free and leaped to the saddle. Wheeling about, they came again into the center of the yard. At that moment Claude and two of the men burst from the barn, yelling as they came.

'Keep low!'

Tom cried his warning at Calico as he twisted around and threw a hasty shot toward the homesteaders.

CHAPTER FIFTEEN

They hammered across the hard pack at a dead gallop.

'The river—head for the river,' Tom shouted at Jones. There would be brush and trees along its bank in which they could disappear and perhaps elude the pursuit that was certain to follow.

A shot gun *blam-blammed* as both its barrels were fired in quick succession. But the two riders were beyond the short range of the weapon. Tom smiled grimly. They were fortunate that it had not been a rifle.

They broke out onto the prairie, leaving the corrals and sheds and shrubbery of the Gillen place behind. The barn was aglow with fire that apparently had gotten beyond control and was sweeping through the structure. Lights now showed in the window of Gillen's house, and men were racing back and forth.

Tom then heard the quick drum of running horses and he realized that some of the homesteaders had chosen to give chase. Bent low over the extended neck of the black as they thundered off through the night, he risked a glance over his shoulder.

Four men were behind them. The fifth, and probably one or two who had been inside the house, were remaining to battle the fire, which was now eating through the roof of the barn and thrusting sharp, yellow tongues toward the sky. Tom felt a pang of remorse as he realized the structure was doomed. He had not planned on destroying it; he had thought the homesteaders would concentrate on the fire and during those moments Calico Jones and he could escape. But it had not worked out that way.

'River ahead.' Calico's voice drifted back to him.

'Cut right,' he shouted back in reply.

He saw the dark wall of brush and trees rushing toward them. Once inside the deep shadows of the grove, it should be easy to lose their pursuers and leave the valley. But it would be best to get as far from Gillen's as possible before they halted. The fire, visible for miles around, would serve as a summons for all the other ranchers and farmers. They would flock to Gillen's quickly and add their support to the search.

He pulled up beside Calico. 'Keep going for another mile or so,' he called. 'When you see a good spot to hide in, sing out.'

Jones nodded. 'Where you goin'?'

Tom held up his captured rifle. 'No place. Just watching our back trail in case somebody draws up too close.'

Calico forged ahead, weaving in and out of the dense brush, following the brief, open lanes between trees, and dipping in and out of the small hollows. Tom gave the black his head and let him run along in the wake of the old puncher's horse. From time to time he glanced to their rear. He caught no glimpse of Claude and the others. Once he heard a sharp pounding and knew it could only be them, but he was unable to determine their exact positions. Somewhere behind, but the sound seemed to arise more off to the side than he expected it to.

He could feel the black beginning to tire. The fast, reckless run through the forest was sapping its strength. And the chances for stumbling were increasing. Tom looked ahead to Calico Jones; they should be pulling off, finding a place in which to hide—and wait.

He saw then they were curving nearer to the river. The shrubbery was becoming more dense, the trees smaller and more plentiful. The horses slowed perceptibly as the growth became a hinderance and Ford flung a quick, worried glance to their back trail. Relief flowed through him when he saw no evidence of the homesteaders.

They plunged on, the crackling and swishing of the brush fearfully loud, it seemed to Ford, and then abruptly they were in a small clearing around which there was a thick wall of shrubbery. Tom heaved a sigh. Calico had known what he was doing; he had led them into a dense thicket.

Ford moved up beside Jones and dismounted. Both horses were near spent and stood with heads down sucking for breath. They could not have maintained the wild pace much farther.

'Reckon we're safe here,' Calico said, squatting on his heels. 'We listen right sharp we ought to hear them go runnin' by.'

'Should be pretty quick,' Ford replied. 'Don't think they're far behind us.'

'You figure this place is good enough?' Jones asked, doubts assailing him suddenly. 'Might be a better spot on closer to the river.'

'This is fine,' Tom assured him. 'If they find us here, they'll find us anywhere.'

They waited in silence after that, with the night broken only by the noisy wheezing of the horses. Five minutes dragged by ... ten ... Claude and his followers should have caught up and passed. Tom stirred uneasily. The thought that the homesteaders had given up and turned back was not believable. They would not have forsaken the chase that soon.

'Something's wrong,' he murmured, rising to his feet. 'I'm going—'

'Hist.' Calico gave out a warning.

Tom listened into the dark. He heard it then, the soft, muted sound of a horse walking slowly over the humus-cushioned floor of the forest. Understanding came quickly to Ford; the homesteaders had lost them when they reached the brush and were now proceeding carefully through the grove in the hope of flushing them into the open.

Ford cast an anxious glance at the horses. If either blew or nickered, their presence would be revealed. Rigid, he rode out the moments, considering his best possible move if they were found. He should try to reach the homesteader first and silence him before he could cry out. Use the rifle as a club. A gunshot was out of the question.

The quiet passage of the homesteader became more distinct. The sound drew abreast, seemed to halt there, then began to fade. Ford drew a full breath and turned his attention toward the river. There should be a man between them and the stream, he reasoned. Claude likely had strung his posse out in a line, sending them prowling through the forest like a foraging party. The chances were good a man would swing around the thicket—but if he happened to know the area well he could conceivably suspect the dense, brushy area to be a perfect place for hiding.

Ford, motioning to Calico for silence, crept to the edge of the thicket and halted. He listened hard into the night. He could hear nothing, and after another five minutes had elapsed, Tom Ford concluded they had given Claude and his riders the slip. He turned back to Jones.

'They've gone on,' he said, keeping his voice down nevertheless. 'Expect we'd better be getting out of here. Soon as they find they've run past us, they'll start doubling back.'

Calico nodded. 'Which way do we head?'

'For Gordon's,' Ford replied, and then frowned. 'There's something that keeps sticking in my head. Back at Gillen's I heard them talking about deeds to the property that had been raided. Whoever's doing it was smart enough to get papers from the people they ran off. Paid a hundred dollars apiece for the titles, it seems.'

'Man would do that if he wanted a clear title.'

'Just what I thought—and if he was that careful he'd record those deeds. So, if we knew who filed the papers we'd know who was behind the whole affair.'

'By jehosphat!' Calico exclaimed. 'You're right! Be the way to prove it ain't Jay Gordon!'

'They kept talking about Gordon, mentioned his name when they spoke of the deeds. Could find out that it's him after all.'

Jones sobered instantly. He was quiet for a long minute. 'Well, that's somethin' I'd sure admire to know,' he said finally, 'they got me about half ways believin' it now.'

'Those deeds would be filed in Capital

City,' Tom said, thinking aloud. Then, directly to Jones, 'How far is it from here?'

'Capital City? Half a day, hard ridin'. Maybe a mite less.'

'Going to crowd us,' Ford said, 'so we both better get started. Here's what we do; you line out for the capitol. Find out who recorded those deeds—if that's what's been done. Get all the information you can, then head for Gordon's.'

'Wish't I had a fresh horse,' Jones said. 'Could ride all night.'

'You'll have to anyway. Stalcup and his crowd will figure we'll hurry to tip Gordon off about the raid they're planning. They'll step things up.'

'Where'll you be?'

'No use trying to talk to Stalcup and the homesteaders; just get myself in the soup again. I'll ride to Gordon's, see if I can get him to listen to me.'

'Goin' to take some doin', considerin' the way he was feelin' last time he saw you.'

'Know that,' Ford agreed. 'Reason why you've got to get back from Capital City fast as possible. I'll try to keep things buttoned down until you show up. Then we'll have the answer.'

'We hope,' Calico said. 'One thing you'd better be watchin' out for when you get to Gordon's—besides Jay himself—is whoever it is that's pullin' these raids. If it's some of the crew who won't want you talkin' to Jay, they'll sure as shootin' try to stop you.'

Ford nodded. 'Same goes for you. When you get back to the ranch, slip in careful.'

'Was just thinkin', maybe I can do some horse swappin' after I get goin'. Ought to be a rancher somewhere between here and Capital City that'll let me trade off for the trip.'

'Bound to be. Which way do you go?'

'Got to ford the river, cut north.'

'Good. Not likely to run into Claude and his bunch.'

'One good thing,' Calico said, 'but I reckon you got more worryin' to do over them than me. They'll be combin' this valley and you'll be crossin' right about the middle.'

'I'll keep my eyes open,' Tom said, walking with the old man to his horse. 'So long—and good luck. See you at Gordon's.'

Calico settled himself on the saddle and looked down at Ford. 'Luck to you, son,' he said, his long face solemn. 'You take care—I want to find you waitin' at the ranch when I get there.'

CHAPTER SIXTEEN

Tom Ford stood quietly in the brush listening to the sounds of Calico Jones riding off toward the river. He felt a lump in his throat and he breathed a silent prayer that the old puncher would encounter no trouble during his journey. In the few hours they had been thrown together Calico had carved a niche for himself in the small gallery of real friends Tom Ford had accepted.

When he could no longer hear Jones, Tom turned to his horse and swung to the saddle. A long and dangerous road lay before him, too, one best covered during the dark hours, and the sooner begun the better his chances for completing it safely.

He walked the black quietly from the thicket into the more open area of the grove. Claude and his men were to the north, he guessed, as he had heard nothing that would indicate they had doubled back. If he could get out of the brushy area and cross the valley unseen by them, half his problems would be solved.

He proceeded with caution, holding the little cow pony to a slow walk, avoiding the dry branches when possible and always keeping in the shadows. An orange glow still hung in the sky over toward Gillen's place.

He hoped that the fire hadn't spread to the other buildings, and again regretted the necessity for it all.

He came to the end of the grove and broke out onto the plains. He halted immediately, his gaze on the flat, starlit-flooded land. A rider would loom up prominently to searching eyes, he realized. It was wiser to stay within the cover of the trees as long as possible. Accordingly, he pulled back into the fringe of brush and continued on toward the north. This presented a new danger—the possibility of running head on into the homesteaders making their return trip. But the gamble was necessary. They most certainly would see him if he struck boldly off across the flats.

He pushed on at a steady pace, swinging to the edge of the trees occasionally to look out over the valley as he endeavored to estimate the proper point at which to cross over. He must be careful to not ride too far north and thus waste time in angling back; he had to reach Gordon's by the shortest possible route.

A short time later he saw a darker smudge off to his right and knew he had come to one of the burned out homesteads that Calico and he had visited earlier. It was time to forsake the shelter of the brush and head east. He halted, thinking of Claude and his men; the fact he had neither seen nor heard anything of them disturbed him. He would have felt better and much safer if he knew their exact position. But that, too, could no longer be a consideration. He must cross the valley and get to Gordon's.

He pulled out of the brush, rode at a trot by the charred ruins of the homestead and soon reached open land. The night was clear and quiet, with the stars lighting his way brightly and a cool breeze slipping in from the south. The black eased into a comfortable lope and followed along a grassy swale that deadened the sound of his hoof beats. The miles began to slip by.

It was a hushed, beautiful world, seemingly far removed from the terrible trouble that hung, like a sword of Damocles, above it. This was no land of violence, of echoing gunshots, of spilled blood and raging fires and death. This was a land of soft starlight, of gentle, soft winds carrying the breath of wild flowers, of muted noises—A universe in which no one thing was at odds with another, in which peace—

'There goes one of them!'

Claude's harsh shout shattered the lulling illusion, sending a burst of alarm through Tom Ford. The homesteaders had outguessed him and had quit the brush ahead of him to search the plains. A gun cracked wickedly through the disrupted silence. Tom heard the angry whine of a bullet close by. He jammed his spurs into the black and sent him plunging ahead.

'Cut him down!' Claude cried. 'Knock him off'n that saddle!'

Ford bent low, his eyes reaching ahead, looking for a deep swale into which he might find safety, a ridge behind which he could flee and escape the oncoming men. It would be easy to turn, to use his rifle, but he was reluctant to do so. He had no real quarrel with Claude and the others. Nor did they have one with him if they only understood. He would not kill unless they forced him into it.

He looked over his shoulder. Claude and his posse were ranged out behind him in a widely spaced line. The black was holding his own with their fresher horses but Tom doubted if he could keep it up for long. He searched ahead again ... a mile yet to the buttes ... a long mile.

The homesteaders opened up with their guns at that moment. He heard the twin blasts of a shotgun, but knew the man was wasting powder and lead. He was far beyond the weapon's reach. But the rifles were something else. Twice he heard the drone of bullets only inches from his head. Twisting about, he pointed his own gun toward the men but aimed high. He would let them know he had a rifle—and would use it if pressed.

Immediately it seemed to him Claude and the posse began to fade back, to lose ground. The gunshot had taken the edge off their determination. He fired a second bullet, this time deliberately placing it nearer their heads. A yell went up but he knew it was from alarm and surprise.

He turned his attention then to the dark, irregular line of bluffs now almost upon him. The black was failing and he was thankful there was only a short distance farther to go, for once in the rough depths of the buttes, it would be simple to shake off the homesteaders.

He reached the first outcropping of rock and brush and raced into it. A narrow canyon opened up to his left and he wheeled into it. The black dropped to a trot, then to a fast walk as he followed its ascending course. Loose rock and shale clattered from beneath his hoofs and once he slid off to the side, but he kept doggedly at it. And then abruptly they were on the top. Ford drew the heaving pony to a stop and looked down into the valley. Claude and the others had turned back and were only dark shadows moving across the land.

Tom Ford sighed. It had been easier than he had expected, but luck had been with him. Had the homesteaders jumped him on the far side of the valley they likely would not have given up so quickly. Here, on the fringe of Gordon's range they probably decided it was wiser not to pursue him too far; there was a good chance other JOG riders were nearby.

He allowed the black to regain his wind and then rode on. He came upon the herd three hours later, but gave it a wide berth.

Shortly after daybreak he crested the ridge that lay west of Gordon's ranch and looked down on the scatter of buildings. Smoke was rising from the kitchen chimney and there were horses, saddled and ready for the day's work, waiting in the corral.

Ford studied the situation for a time endeavoring to figure out his best means of approach. He came finally to a decision; he would simply ride in. If he were lucky he would get to Jay Gordon without being interrupted. If halted, he would demand to be taken to the rancher and make such an issue of it that he would not be denied. Attempting to sneak in, he knew, would be an open invitation for a bullet.

He came down the slope at an easy trot, his hammering pulse belying the outward calm that cloaked his rigid shape. He reached the yard and rode across the area separating the main house from the crew's quarters. His throat began to tighten as tension closed in on him. The hired hands, he saw, were in the dining room, having their morning meal.

Moving past the door, he heard a chair scrape suddenly against the floor. Someone had noticed him. He kept his face straight ahead. Another ten yards to the corner of the house, then he would be in front of the building and moving to the hitchrack. If he could get that far—

'Hold it, mister!'

Bill Tusas's voice was a sharp stab of sound in the hush.

Ford slowed. He considered making a quick dash for the corner, but thought better of it. Tusas would not hesitate to shoot. He came to a complete halt and wheeled about. Tusas, a gun in his hand and flanked by a half-a-dozen of the crew, stood just outside the door.

'Whatever business we've got, Bill, can wait,' Tom said in a voice that carried. 'Right now I've got to talk to Gordon. There's trouble coming—from the homesteaders and ranchers west of here.'

Tusas stalked deeper into the yard. 'Gordon don't want to see you. Said so. Now, climb down off that horse.'

Ford shook his head. 'Important I see Gordon. I figure to do just that.'

'Nope,' Tusas answered. 'His orders was to take you in to the marshal. And that's what I'm goin' to do.'

A trip I'd never finish, Tom thought, but he said nothing. Several of the crew sauntered farther into the yard. Poe, Chesser, Joe Sharpe. Ford watched them fan out from Tusas's sides. Others drifted off toward the bunkhouse, anxious to keep out of harm's way. Quint Magee was nowhere to be seen.

'You climbin' down or am I pullin' you off that saddle?' Tusas asked softly.

'Stay out of this, Bill,' Tom answered. 'We'll settle our trouble later.'

Chesser and Poe moved in suddenly from opposite points. They had drawn their guns and had the hammers pulled back ready to fire. Tusas, grinning broadly at Ford, holstered his own weapon.

'Keep him covered, boys,' he said with a broad wink. 'This is goin' to pleasure me some—helpin' the drifter off his horse.'

'Wait!'

The voice of Susan Gordon, coming from the corner of the porch, halted Tusas in his tracks. Ford swung a surprised glance at her. This was a different Susan from the one he had met before. Her face was determined, her lips compressed into a tight line, and sparks danced in her eyes. She now wore a corduroy riding skirt, dark colored blouse and boots, and in her hands she held a carbine. There was nothing cowed or timid about this new Susan Gordon.

'Get away from him,' she ordered, her tone brisk and businesslike.

Poe and Chesser did not move. Tusas flung her a contemptuous look. 'Keep out of the way, lady. I'm doin' what your pa said.'

'I don't care what he said,' she snapped. 'Stand back!'

Chesser swiveled his attention to Tusas. The squat cowboy shook his head. 'Don't pay her no mind.'

The rifle in Susan's hands lifted slightly. It cracked. Dust spurted over Tusas's feet. He yelled and jumped to one side.

'All of you—go on about your work,' the girl said evenly. 'This man wants to see my father. I intend to see that he does. If we need someone to take him in to town, I'll send for you.'

Tusas's face was a bright red. Ford grinned at him, then stepped down from the black. He shouldered by Chesser and walked to where Susan waited.

'My father's in his office,' she said without looking at him. 'Go ahead.'

He reached down for the carbine. 'Lead the way. I'll follow you.'

She shook off his hand. 'No. I've been years working up to this. I'll see it through.'

CHAPTER SEVENTEEN

Ford stared at Susan's set features. 'Better pull back onto the porch,' he murmured. 'Never a good idea to press your luck too far.'

She nodded, backed slowly around the corner and came to a halt on the gallery. She leaned up against the wall, suddenly all woman again. Inside the house Jay Gordon was shouting for her, for Magee, for somebody—for anybody. Tom looked more closely at the girl.

'What do you mean, you've been working up to this? To what?'

'To being someone around here, around my own home, besides just a stick of furniture—and a servant.'

Tom frowned. He stepped off the porch, crossed to the corner of the house and glanced into the yard. Tusas and a half-a-dozen more riders had collected in front of their quarters and were talking among themselves. Ford hurried back to the girl.

'You bluffed them out,' he said, smiling. 'They've moved on. Now, what's this all about?'

Susan shrugged her slim shoulders. 'You're new around here so of course you don't know about things. I never meant much to my father when my brother was alive. Just someone to boss around, to shout at and keep the house straight and meals on time. No one, not even the hired hands, paid any attention to me. I was just tolerated.

'When Jock was killed I thought matters might change, that my father and I would grow closer together. Instead, it has been worse. He was never an easy man to get along with and Jock's death turned him into a tyrant. The only men he could get to work for him were the ones like Bill Tusas and a few of the old hands who were too old to move on and had to stay.'

'Like Calico Jones and Cletus.'

'Yes, like them, and Quint Magee. Quint will stay and take my father's ranting and raving regardless. He thinks that much of the ranch.'

'He could have other reasons,' Ford said quietly.

Susan looked at him curiously, but let it pass. 'Yesterday when you were here, you sort of brought matters to a head for me. You're the first man I ever saw defy my father, and I guess I sort of took courage from that. Last night we had words. And then this morning when I heard you talking to Tusas and I listened to his answers, I decided it was time to take another step—to show Bill Tusas and the others—'

'You did,' Tom interrupted gently. 'And I'm obliged to you. Don't think they're over their surprise yet. But I've got to talk to Gordon—to your father. There's serious trouble coming.'

'Can't you tell me?'

'We're short on time,' he said. 'Be better if we went in to your father...' He paused. It was important to her that she know, he realized.

He gave her the facts as he knew them, moving quickly over the details. When he had concluded, she smiled at him.

'Thank you, Tom,' she said, and turned toward the door. Again she halted and placed her hand on his arm. 'One more thing ... Jock—you weren't the one who—'

'No,' Ford said, 'it wasn't me. You've got my word for that.'

'I never thought so,' she said and moved on. They entered the house, crossed the parlor and turned into Gordon's office. The rancher, his face sullen with anger, sat in his wheelchair beside the desk. He glanced up at her as she appeared in the doorway.

'Where the devil you been, girl?'

'My name is Susan,' she replied calmly. 'We went over that last night.'

'All right—Susan! What was that gunshot?'

The question died on Gordon's lips as Tom Ford stepped into view. He swore, spun his chair about and grabbed for a pistol hanging in a holster on the wall behind the desk. Ford was a breath ahead of him. He jerked the weapon from its leather pocket and tossed it into a chair across the room. Gordon whirled around, his eyes flaming.

'You've got a hell of a lot of nerve,' he gritted in a savage tone, 'coming here like this. And you—' he added, throwing his glance at Susan, 'you—my own flesh and blood—my own daughter.'

'You never gave that much thought before,' she said coolly.

'Makes no difference! He murdered your own brother, your own kin.'

'He says he didn't. I believe him.'

'You believe him! You'd take his word.'

'Happens to be the truth,' Ford cut in. 'Whether you think so or not. But that's not why I'm here. You've got trouble coming your way.'

'Trouble!' Gordon echoed. 'What's that mean? What kind of trouble?'

'There's a posse of homesteaders and ranchers on their way to burn you out.'

'Burn me out!' Gordon shouted. 'What're you giving me, Ford? What're you up to?'

'Nothing,' Tom said. 'Somebody's been carrying on raids in the valley west of your range. Been several places burned to the ground and the people driven off. They figure you're behind it.'

'Me? They're crazy! Had nothing to do with it and any man says I have is a liar! I've got no use for any of that stinking, starve-out bunch, but I've never laid a hand on any of them or their property. What the devil makes them think it was me?'

'Raiders all rode horses wearing your JOG brand ... You telling me you've never heard about it before?'

Gordon squirmed impatiently in his chair. 'Course I've heard it before. From several places. Dorsett mentioned it to me once, but I never paid no mind. Man builds himself up a spread like mine, he gets sniped at from all sides.'

'Gone past that now. These people from west of here are convinced it's all your doing, and they'll be coming to settle. Man by the name of Stalcup at the head.'

'Stalcup—a two-bit lawyer that moved into this country a few years back.'

'Point is,' Tom broke in quietly, 'are you behind it?'

Jay Gordon almost raised himself from his chair. His hands gripped the metal arms so tightly his knuckles went dead white. His face swelled and reddened until it seemed about to burst.

'No—goddamnit—no! I've got nothing to do with it. And the man who says I did—'

Ford nodded. 'That's what Calico and I figured. But somebody is, and they're using your brand as a cover.'

Silence followed Tom's words, a hush broken only by Gordon's quick, angry breathing. Susan said, finally, 'You think it's somebody that works for us?'

'Can't be sure,' Ford said. 'But we'll soon know. Calico rode on to Capital City. Whoever it is took deeds from the homesteaders and small ranchers after forcing them to sell. Those deeds will have to be recorded. Once we know whose name they're recorded under, we'll have the answer.'

'Then all we've got to do is tell that to Stalcup and his crowd when they show up,' Gordon said, his tone now more subdued.

'No, we'll have to wait until Calico gets here. If we show our hand too soon we could get Calico ambushed, like Gillen.'

'Gillen? Who's that?'

'That rancher who was on his way to see you but caught a rifle bullet in his back before he got here.'

Gordon said. 'The one you claimed you found and packed in.'

'That's the way it was. Somebody else bushwhacked him.'

'I ain't so sure,' Gordon said arbitrarily. 'And I ain't so sure I buy this tale of yours about the squatters and ranchers. Could be you've got some reason for stirring all this up. And you've got no call to do me any favors—not unless you're trying to make up for something.'

Tom shook his head. 'I'm not trying to make up for anything,' he said patiently. 'There's no reason to. Just don't want to see trouble like this get started. Been through a couple of range wars myself and I—'

'Oh, sure,' Gordon said sarcastically. 'You're everybody's friend, a real do-gooder.'

'No!' Susan exclaimed, taking a step toward Gordon. 'It's not that! It's something you don't understand—never did and never will. You're so wrapped up in your own self, your own feelings and convictions that you can't see how any man can be a friend to another—stranger or not!'

'Now, wait a minute—'

'No, you wait!' Susan's eyes flashed and her cheeks glowed with angry color. 'You've never had a friend! You don't know what the word means. You can't understand how one man, even at the risk of his life, could turn aside to help another simply because right is right, and wrong is wrong. You can't believe it is possible because you've always surrounded yourself with people who toadied to you, yet who wouldn't care if you—'

'All right, Susan!' Gordon roared. 'That will be enough! I'm getting a bit tired of your preaching.'

'Listen to her,' Tom Ford said. 'What she says—'

'And listen to you, too, eh? Well, far as I'm concerned nothing between us has changed. I still think you're who I figure you are—the man who murdered my son. Maybe be something to this homesteader's bellyaching and I'll straighten it out, but you're siding me for a reason, not because you're everybody's friend as my daughter seems to think. I'm handing you over to Dorsett—'

A shotgun suddenly blasted in the yard fronting the house. Henry Stalcup's voice came through the open doorway.

'Gordon! Jay Gordon! Come out!'

CHAPTER EIGHTEEN

Ford, wheeling swiftly, hurried to the window of the parlor. Susan crowded up beside him. Gordon followed.

Stalcup, flanked by Claude and another man, had halted a few yards beyond the hitchrack. Sitting quietly on their horses just outside the gate were ten more riders. Each was armed with a shotgun or rifle. Only Stalcup held no weapon.

Tom turned to Gordon. 'It's your move.'

The rancher's jaw shot forward to a hard, jutting angle. He gave the wheels of his chair a thrust and propelled himself out onto the porch. Susan and Ford closed in behind him. He glanced angrily over the assembled men, then brought his attention back to Stalcup.

'What do you want?'

Quint Magee and Cletus Todd, apparently just returning from some errand, were trotting up from the corral. In front of the bunkhouse Bill Tusas and several more of the crew had pulled into a short line.

'Talk,' Stalcup said. 'First thing, you'd better tell your boys to stand easy. I've got ten more men besides the ones you're looking at.'

'They'll do nothing unless you start it,' Gordon snapped.

Ford watched Magee and Todd come to a halt at the edge of the porch. The homesteaders had moved faster than he had expected. He had hoped Calico would return before the clash occurred but that had been a useless wish; the moment was at hand.

'Say what you've got to say and get off my land,' Gordon said, as he rolled himself up to the front of the gallery.

'You know what we're here for,' Stalcup replied. 'Your man there has told you by now.'

'He don't work for me.'

'I know better than that. He was over in the valley last night. Him and another one, snooping around. We caught them but they slipped through our fingers after they set fire to Gillen's barn.'

Gordon turned his head, frowned, and glanced at Tom. Ford said, 'Had to do it. Was the only way Calico and I could escape. Didn't expect them to let the fire get out of control.'

'All right, he was there,' Gordon said. 'What's that got to do with it?'

'We're finished with letting you run over us,' Stalcup said. 'I'm here to make you a peaceable offer. Give us back the deeds to the places you took over and your word to stay out of the valley and we'll call it quits. Otherwise—'

'Otherwise what?'

'We'll burn every building on this place to the ground!'

'You or any man with you makes a move toward this house and he's dead!' Gordon shouted. 'And I don't know what you're talking about. There's been no raids by any of my crew. And I've got no deeds!'

'We know better, Gordon,' Stalcup broke in. 'We have the proof!'

'You're a damn liar!' the rancher exploded, his face livid. 'I've got no use for you and your bunch—but I never harmed any of you, same as I've never wanted a foot of your land. Now, turn around and ride out of here or I'm cutting my boys loose!'

'All right,' Stalcup shouted angrily. 'Just

remember, this is on your head! We're willing to talk.'

Tom Ford pushed by Gordon and stepped out into the yard. He threw a glance toward Magee and Cletus Todd, to Tusas and those watching silently from the bunkhouse, then brought his eyes back to Stalcup and the men who flanked him.

'Hold up here a minute!' he said, his voice low and calm but reaching to the farthest rider. 'There's no call to spill blood. I told you yesterday, Stalcup, Gordon has nothing to do with your trouble. And I can prove that if you'll give me a little time.'

'Prove it? How?' Stalcup demanded, his tone filled with doubt and mistrust.

Tom hesitated. It would still be dangerous to explain Calico's mission. He could not risk the life of the old man. 'Can't tell you yet. Just give me some time.'

Ford felt Susan move up to his shoulder. 'We don't want trouble, Mr Stalcup,' she said. 'Regardless of what my father said, we want this straightened out peacefully. All we ask is a couple of hours.'

'Don't beg him!' Jay Gordon yelled from the porch. 'By God, if he can't take my word for it, let him crack his whip! Then we'll see who comes out on top of the pile!'

'By counting the dead men on each side—that way you mean?' Ford said icily, turning to the rancher. 'That how you tell?'

134

'I don't ask favors of nobody,' Gordon declared. 'Never have and I don't aim to start now.'

'How about it, Stalcup?' Tom asked, coming back to the homesteader.

'Don't see any point in holding off. Can't talk sense to Gordon there, and we've put this thing off long enough.'

Claude, a few paces to the left of Stalcup, moved up to the man and said something to him in an urgent, anxious manner. Stalcup appeared to listen, then shook his head violently. Suddenly his hand darted inside his coat. He whipped out a revolver and threw a shot directly at Jay Gordon.

For the merest fragment of time Tom Ford stood rooted to the ground while the full meaning of Stalcup's actions hammered at him. *The fool—he's lit the fuse for sure now!* That thought sent Ford into swift action. He drew his weapon, fired a hasty bullet at Stalcup, who, with Claude and the other man was racing madly for the gate. Guns began to rattle and Tom heard the solid thud of lead smashing into the walls of the house and saw small geysers of dust lift where bullets fell short and plowed into the ground.

He spun and pushed Susan before him, shielding her with his own bulk. They reached the porch. 'Inside!' he shouted, seizing Gordon's wheelchair and pivoting it toward the door.

'Get me my gun!' the rancher yelled. 'By God, I'll show they they can't come barging onto a man's place.'

Ford paid no attention. Aided by Susan he rolled Gordon into the house. 'Shut this door—lock it!' he said sharply, as he came back out onto the porch. Magee and Cletus Todd were crouched against the wall shooting irregularly at the homesteaders, who were now spreading out to form a circle around the yard. Stalcup had said there were ten more men somewhere; Tom could see no signs of them but they could be hidden in the brush.

He glanced toward the bunkhouse. Tusas and the others had fled inside. He could see faces at the windows peering out. They would be no help there. Stalcup and his men would close in from all sides.

Ford swung toward Magee and Todd.

'Stay here,' he said. 'Don't let them get in close—and watch for torches.'

He heard Magee say something in reply but he was already running for the bunkhouse and the foreman's words were lost. He reached the squat, lengthy building and burst through the doorway. Tusas, Poe and half-a-dozen more of the crew turned to face him.

'Get outside!' he ordered. 'You won't do any good in here. Scatter through the yard, get behind the sheds and corrals. They'll hit us from all directions.'

'Who the hell are you to be givin' orders?' Tusas demanded, pushing forward.

Ford jammed his gun barrel into Tusas's belly, and shoved him toward the door. 'We'll talk about it later,' he said.

Tusas, surprised and off balance, stumbled out into the yard. Ford wheeled to the others and immediately they followed. They halted in a group, uncertain of their next move. A splatter of gunshots echoed through the warm morning air. Bullets thunked into the wall of the bunkhouse and a window shattered with a loud crash. Instantly the men separated and bent low, running for cover.

'Watch for fire!' Tom yelled after them.

Dirt spewed over his feet. He threw himself to one side and ducked behind a clump of lilac. Two riders were racing in from the low hill beyond the feed barn. One had a rifle to his shoulder and was shooting as he rode. The other, a yard behind, carried a stick from the tip of which an oil-soaked rag burned furiously.

Tom took careful aim at the man with the torch, and squeezed off a shot. The homesteader yelled, dropped the flaming firebrand, and curved off. Ford sent a second bullet at the man's partner, saw him rock on the saddle and claw at the horn to steady himself. Then the rider turned back.

The firing began to pick up. Tom could hear the hard pound of running horses on the far side of the house and hoped someone had taken a stand in that area. The entire south wall of the building might be exposed and unprotected. He decided he could not gamble on it. Keeping low, he spurted from the shelter of the lilac and sprinted across the yard. He reached the near corner of the house, and found Curly Sheppard, one of Gordon's older riders, hunkered down there, a rifle, smoke trickling from its muzzle, in his hands.

Tom grinning at him, rushed on. He gained the opposite corner, then drew to a halt. The shooting had dwindled again. He could see no men along that side of the house, and he started to turn back to get Sheppard and one or two others and station them along the wall. Henry Stalcup appeared suddenly off to his left. Ford halted and dropped to his knees behind a clump of brush. He watched Stalcup ride cautiously toward a small tool shed standing at the extreme edge of the yard.

Tom brought up his gun, then thought better of it. There was something in Stalcup's manner that puzzled him. He allowed the man to continue, then, bent low and keeping the posts of a holding pen between Stalcup and himself, he circled around and came in behind the shed. Tom saw the dark shape of a second man emerge from the shadows.

'Stalcup—here.'

The voice was that of Bill Tusas. Ford, still crouched, pressed up hard against the rough boards of the shed. He heard Stalcup bring his horse to a stop.

'What the hell you up to?' Tusas demanded in a harsh tone. 'You tryin' to get me and the boys killed?'

'Couldn't help it,' Stalcup answered. 'There was no holding them back.'

'Should've let me know. You've got us caught in the middle.'

'Work toward the barn,' Stalcup said. 'I'll pull everybody away from there. You can ease out...'

Tom Ford listened in amazed silence as the truth dawned slowly upon him. Stalcup was the man behind the raids! Stalcup, masquerading as the homesteader's friend, acting as their spokesman, was the mastermind behind the land steal!

And Bill Tusas and his crowd were in it with him. Poe, Sharpe, Hugh Chesser, possibly others. Either they were partners in the scheme or else Stalcup had simply hired them to raid the valley, terrorize the settlers and force them to terms. That was how the JOG branded horses came into the picture.

An oath slipped from Tom Ford's lips. He rose to his feet. If he acted quickly there was a chance he could stop the fight before too many men were hurt. His gun ready, he moved swiftly around the shed and stepped into the open.

'Raise your hands,' he said in a voice that trembled with anger, 'Or I'll kill you both!'

CHAPTER NINETEEN

Stalcup stiffened perceptibly, his body jarring sharply as though struck. Tusas, his face turned away, his shoulders hunched, moved his arms slightly.

'Don't try it, Bill,' Ford warned softly. 'You'll be dead before you can clear leather.'

Tusas relaxed carefully. Not taking his eyes from the pair, Tom called, 'Sheppard—come here!'

Immediately there was the quick pound of running feet. The old puncher appeared at the corner of the shed, paused, then stared at Stalcup and Tusas.

'What's goin' on?'

'Seems we've got to the bottom of all the trouble,' Tom said. 'Hold a gun on them. If either one makes a move, shoot.'

Sheppard said, 'Sure, you bet.'

Ford motioned to Stalcup. 'Get down,' he commanded in a flat, uncompromising voice.

Stalcup came off his horse, steadying himself with one hand, holding the other above his head. He halted beside Tusas. Tom stepped in behind the two men and relieved them of their pistols.

'Now move,' he said, shoving them both toward the yard. 'You've got some talking to do.'

Tusas stumbled, caught himself. 'You'll never make it,' he said in a hard, promising way. 'One of my boys will cut you down.'

'You better hope he doesn't,' Ford cut in, 'because I'll take you with me. Goes for you, too, Stalcup,' he added. 'When we get into the open you both play it safe. Sing out—tell your men to hold their fire.'

'I—I can't stop them—' Stalcup began and then fell silent.

They reached the hard packed area that lay between the two larger houses. The shooting had ceased entirely and Ford knew they had been spotted by both factions.

'Now's the time,' he murmured. 'You first, Stalcup.'

He responded quickly. 'Don't shoot!' he yelled.

'Tell them to put away their guns and come in. Tell them it's all over.'

Stalcup complied instantly. Ford nudged Tusas with the barrel of his pistol. 'Your turn, Bill.'

Tusas hesitated momentarily. Tom jabbed

the man viciously. Tusas swore, then, 'Poe—Chesser—rest of you boys! Put your guns up!'

'Tell them to get inside the bunkhouse and stay there.'

Tusas repeated the order. 'Keep going,' Ford said when it was done. 'Now we'll talk to Gordon.'

They circled the ranchhouse and came up to the porch. Homesteaders were drifting into the yard slowly, one and two at a time. Somewhere, beyond the barn, a horse was coming in on the run. Tom halted his party in front of Gordon's door. He threw a glance over his shoulder.

'Claude!' he called. 'Come up here. Want you in on this.'

The squat homesteader separated himself from the others and advanced warily. He eyed Ford with distrust. 'This some kind of a trick?'

'No trick. Just want you to find out first hand who's been giving you and your friends all the trouble.'

Claude's lower jaw dropped. 'You mean Henry—Henry Stalcup?'

'He's the one,' Tom said, knocking on the door. It opened at once. He motioned to Tusas and Stalcup. 'Inside.'

They filed into the parlor, Claude and Sheppard bringing up the rear. Jay Gordon, pistol in his hand, watched in fuming silence.

Susan stood a pace behind him. Her eyes caught those of Tom Ford and she gave him a quick smile.

'Here's the cause of all the shooting,' Ford said, motioning Stalcup and Tusas back against the wall. 'Stalcup is the one who's been buying up the land in the valley after Tusas and some others forced the settlers to sign the deeds—probably left blank for him to fill in later.'

Henry Stalcup shrugged and shook his head. 'You can't prove that,' he said quietly. 'It's a put-up job. Maybe Tusas had something to do with the raids, but I—'

Bill Tusas whirled on the man. 'Don't go pushin' any blame off on me! I had nothin' to do with it.'

The door swung open. Calico Jones, dust covered, his clothing sweat soaked, his face sagging with weariness, stepped into the room. He glanced about, then moved to Ford's elbow.

'Got the dope, Tom, but looks like you don't need it. Stalcup's the ranny that's been raisin' all the ruckus. Filed three deeds up there last month.'

'That's a lie,' Stalcup said, still calm and outwardly unperturbed. 'You won't find my name on any deeds, and I defy you to produce even one!'

'Maybe not exactly,' Calico said. 'Deeds was all made out to a H. S. Waggener. But the description of this feller Waggener fits you to a smidgin!'

Stalcup stiffened. Some of the confidence faded from his bearing. 'Still don't prove—'

Understanding came to Tom Ford. 'Expect it does,' he said. 'H. S. Waggener—that's your full name. You just dropped the Waggener part so nobody in the valley would know it was you. Be no problem getting the clerk who handled the deeds at Capital City to identify you if you try squirming out of it.'

Jay Gordon found his voice. 'Now, you see!' he roared, turning upon Claude. 'Coming here, raising all this hell when it was one of your own bunch! You better be a mite careful.'

'What else was we to think?' the homesteader shot back. 'Tusas there, works for you. And he and the rest were ridin' your horses.'

'Weren't doing it on my orders! Didn't know a damn thing about it. Was up to my foreman to see—'

'No difference now,' Ford broke in, halting the angry exchange before it got out of hand and too much was said. 'It's a matter for the law from here on. Claude, we'll leave it up to you and the rest of your people to take them in to Marshal Dorsett and Prairie Grove. Besides all the things that happened in the valley, there's the murder of

Gillen—to—'

'You ain't takin' me nowhere!' Tusas yelled and plunged across the room.

He snatched the pistol from Gordon's hands and spun around to face Ford. Tom, reacting instinctively, drew as he threw himself to one side. Both guns blasted as one, filling the small room with a deafening explosion and a thick, choking cloud of smoke.

'Tom!' Susan screamed through the smothering haze.

Ford pulled himself upright. 'I'm all right,' he answered. His nerves were taut as piano wire, but his muscles were lax and a long coolness was flowing through him as he strained to see through the fog.

'Open that door!' Gordon shouted from his corner. 'Let some of this damn smoke out.'

Calico Jones pulled the panel wide. A voice from the yard called, 'What happened? What's goin' on in there?'

'All over,' the old puncher replied. 'Just keep your saddles.'

The room began to clear. Tusas lay against the wheel of Gordon's chair. Ford stepped to the man's side, bent down and examined him quickly. Bill Tusas was dead. Ford straightened up and felt Susan's hand slip into his own.

'Oh, Tom—I was afraid—'

'It's all right now,' he said. 'Calico, you and Sheppard take care of Bill's body.' He turned to Claude. 'Take your prisoner and move out. Been enough trouble around here for one day. You'll find the rest of Tusas's bunch in the bunkhouse.'

From the porch someone said, 'Three men just rode off from there a few minutes ago.'

'Get after them,' Claude snapped. 'We want 'em all!'

The homesteader wheeled to Stalcup, took him by the arm and pushed him toward the door. 'Let's go, Henry. You got a date with the hangman, soon's we get them deeds straightened out.'

On the gallery Claude halted and looked back at Tom. 'We're obliged to you, friend,' he said, and then to Jay Gordon, 'reckon we're mighty sorry this all come up.'

'Being sorry don't mean anything to me!' the rancher shot back. 'Just get off my land and stay off! And far as you're concerned,' he added, swinging his angry eyes to Ford, 'nothing's changed between us, either! You can—'

'Tom,' Calico Jones called from the end of the gallery. 'Somebody here lookin' for you.'

Ford frowned, stepped to the doorway and glanced out. His heart came to a full and sudden stop. The rider sitting on a tall bay smiling at him in that peculiar, crooked manner could be only one man.

His brother—Fresno.

CHAPTER TWENTY

Tom's first reaction was one of joy. At last the long search was over—he had found Fresno. And then the deeper implications of Fresno's presence on the Gordon spread came to him. Any hopes of making his peace with the rancher would die now. He had planned to take Magee to Colorado, find witnesses, prove to Gordon he was not the man who had killed his son.

'Hear you been looking for me, kid,' Fresno said, swinging off the bay.

He had changed little, Tom noted. A bit heavier, huskier. His face had altered most. A sort of stillness lay upon it and his eyes, once carefree and laughing, were now steady, almost flat. He was well-dressed in expensive broadcloth, which contrasted to the old, smoothly worn gun that hung low on his hip.

'Brother?' Jay Gordon's voice came from the doorway. 'He call you brother?'

Tom ignored the question and walked slowly to the edge of the porch. He could forget Susan, forget JOG and all the rest of the fine dream that had been budding inside his heart. One glance at Fresno, and Jay Gordon would recognize his calling, would swiftly put two and two together and draw his conclusions.

And Fresno, being the sort of man he was, would deny nothing. There it would end. Gordon the bitter, the unforgiving would make no allowances. The brother of the man who had killed his son Jock would be equally condemned.

'Was in Sutterstown a few days ago,' Fresno said, moving up to the gallery. He walked with an easy, fluid grace, slow, yet with a subtle efficiency that governed each motion of his body. 'Bartender there said you were asking for me. Tracked you down from there. Something special on your mind, kid?'

Tom shrugged wearily. Although the thought of returning to a drudging existence in the Polk County hills no longer appealed to him, he said, 'There was ... Pa's dead now ... Figured you might want to come back to Missouri—to the farm.'

'No thanks,' Fresno said with a dry smile. 'No farming for me—and I'm not the settling down kind.' He glanced around the yard. 'What was all the shooting I heard?'

'Just a little mistake,' Tom replied. 'Wait until I get my horse. I'll ride out with you.'

'Not yet you won't!' Jay Gordon boomed from the doorway. 'Not until I get something straight.'

The rancher wheeled himself out onto the porch. He again held the pistol Bill Tusas had wrenched from his hand earlier.

'I hear you say you're Tom's brother?'

Fresno nodded. 'I am.'

'You ever up around Creede—in Colorado?'

'Sure. Plenty of times.'

Tom drifted a step to one side, to where he could come between the two men and block any gunplay.

The rancher said, 'You ever run into anybody up there by the name of Gordon?'

Fresno's brow pulled into a frown. 'Gordon ... Gordon ... Yes, seems I recollect the name from somewhere.'

'Maybe a boy you killed—shot down in cold blood?'

Fresno Ford came to quiet attention. His eyes closed down to narrow slits. 'Reckon that was it,' he said softly. 'A shooting—but not exactly the way you put it.'

'You murdered him! You shot him down in cold blood! I know how it was—sent my foreman up there to look after things. He told me so.'

'Your foreman's a liar,' Fresno said coldly.

'Like hell!' Gordon shouted. 'He'd not tell me anything that wasn't—'

Quint Magee appeared at the corner of the house. He moved forward slowly and halted in front of the rancher.

'Guess I didn't give you the straight of it, Mr Gordon,' he said in a low voice. 'Knowing how you felt about the boy, how you set such store by him, I just didn't have the heart to tell you the truth.'

'The truth! What's that mean?' Gordon demanded.

'Jock was no good—a bad one. He was in a half a dozen scrapes up there. He tried to rob Ford, they told me. Slipped in on him while he was sleeping. Had a knife and would have killed Ford if he hadn't got Jock with the bullet first... There was witnesses.' Magee halted, then glanced up. 'I'm sorry, Mr Gordon. I only wanted...'

Jay Gordon sat as a man stricken, as one turned to stone. His eyes reached out over the heads of the silent men that faced him and were lost somewhere in the rolling land beyond the gate of the mighty spread he had hoped one day his son would command.

'Papa,' Susan's murmur was loud in the hush. 'Papa.'

Gordon seemed to wilt at the sound of her voice. His shoulders went down, his head sagged forward on his breast. The pistol slipped from his fingers and fell to the plank floor of the porch.

'I'm all right—daughter,' he said. 'I'm all right.'

He placed his hands on the wheels of his

chair and turned about slowly. His glance caught that of Tom Ford's. He halted.

'I'm not a man afraid to admit I was wrong,' he said. 'Like to have you stay around—if you don't have any other plans.'

Tom looked at Susan and saw the brightness in her eyes, the smile on her lips. 'I've got no other plans,' he said.

1
rc to ba 12.15

NNS/NFFS   NC

DISCARDED
BAKER CO. PUBLIC LIBRARY